double edge sword

double edge sword

david c williams

Writer's Showcase
San Jose New York Lincoln Shanghai

Writer's Showcase
an imprint of iUniverse, Inc.

For information address:
iUniverse, Inc.
5220 S. 16th St., Suite 200
Lincoln, NE 68512
www.iuniverse.com

Library of Congress catalog card number 94-092297.
for contact information, Creative Thoughts c/o D. C. Williams,
at 4624 W. Northgate Dr., Suite #172 Irving, TX zip 75062,
email address Dcwdes@aol.com

ISBN: 0-595-20985-8

Printed in the United States of America

Chapter One

Now that I've successfully achieved the goals of my dreams, I sit in my recliner and reflect on a particular decade of time. It was a time that impacted me, and our nation, like the resounding rolling thunder that's produced from a mid-summer's storm. During this span of time, I, along with many others of the world, witnessed the shootings of many humanitarian leaders, the war in Vietnam, and a rampant abuse of people's civil rights. In a number of ways, these were very trying times, when finding equality among men seemed as rare as discovering buried treasure. Yet, as a result of the unique travails of this era, many good things managed to eventually transpire. In retrospect, I'd like to think that I might have helped make some of those good things come to pass.

In the early years of the 1960's, my world revolved from within the borderlines of a fast paced city. It's located on the southwestern tip of the state of Tennessee and touches the rhythmic, flowing waters that dance along the shores of the mighty Mississippi River. Memphis was a good place to live in, for both the young and old. In those days, it had been twice recognized as the cleanest city in the state, and was internationally renowned for being the home of a soulful music called the, "blues." On any given night of the week, blues music could be heard echoing throughout the streets. Although the city was nicked named, "The Home of the Blues," that old river front town wasn't blue at all. For me, at the age of 15, it was a happy town that gave me a chance to experience life in a city that was on the rise.

These were also times when some people, white and black, felt they needed to keep themselves and their lives as a separate society. Indirectly, our city responded by finding a way to oblige both cultures. In our fine and prosperous city, special attention had been given to ensure that recreational, spiritual and other social needs for both groups could be addressed. The two cultures were provided with separate or customized amenities for special events. Each had amenities, like their own exclusive movie theaters, restaurants, churches, community center gymnasiums and much more. Both also held their own annual special affairs, like carnivals and parades. Plus, each group maintained and supported the local corner grocery stores, banks and the efforts of other entrepreneur's through out their area. Basically, Black and White people had their own city within the city. A method was also designed that allowed the cultures a chance to share together in some events that periodically came to town. To make those events possible, and still comply with our nation's segregation laws, our towns entertainment halls and arenas had fashioned their establishments with an interior decor to include curtains, partitions and other types of room dividers that would keep the two races separate as they enjoyed the events together. However, the best part about our city was living among my race of people. We had thriving communities that linked from the neighborhoods of the inner city, and into the suburban areas, solidifying a village township in unity. Our village communities were positive places for us to grow, and as a whole, we were all protected by the wisdom from the adage that says, "There is safety in numbers."

During my youth, I was a pretty good kid, an average teenager that might climb a tree to see how high a boy could climb, or sometimes, a mannish boy just trying to grow up too fast. Although unfortunately, and much sooner than I would've desired, both the good and the mischievous kid that existed inside of me would experience a reality check.

In these times of so much social confusion, innocently, I'd never assumed that the separation of the races was a mandated issue, simply a mere matter of people just preferring to be with their own friends, like me and my homeboys. But, my world, in that southern town by the shore of that slow moving muddy Mississippi river, was about to reveal it's dark side to me. My town was about to show me that her true colors, on the segregation legislation, were of a bias and camouflaging nature.

As I was walking through the halls of E. K. Waymon High School, one of my homeboys, Homer Jones, waved his hand high in the air to get my attention, "Wait up, brother J." he said, while coming towards me. "Are we gonna play some basketball after school?"

"Sure we're gonna play, but when did you learn the game?"

"Ha, ha.' Homer sarcastically replied. "If you trying to be funny, it ain't working. Anyway, when I get this hook shot down, ain't nobody gonna control my game."

"That's right brother, keep the faith and keep on dreaming. The game's gonna start about 4:00 p.m. I'm gonna be a little late, but you need to hang around until I get there. That way you can take some notes and learn a little something about what to do with a basketball."

In his own defense, Homer announces, "Sounds like you need to ask somebody, obviously ain't nobody told you. I'm the fastest fat man to ever hit the courts."

"Ha, ha! We'll see how many points your fat self can score, at four. But right now, I've got to go. Stay tuned, and I'll see you soon."

We gave each other a high-five slap, as he said, "Later brother. I'll see you on the court."

I continued through the school's halls and made my way outside towards the route that led me to a short cut home. It had been a good day; I'd aced all of my school tests and felt like they should've bumped me up a couple of grades. I was confident in my abilities and really didn't think that they had a test in that whole school that I couldn't just breeze through. But on this particular day, a test of another sort was ahead of me.

My short cut followed a stretch of railroad tracks, and to get to the other side of those tracks, I jumped between two rail cars that were sitting by a side door of an old wood processing plant. That's when I encountered another boy. He was about my age and posed no threat, but he was in my way. So, my defensive attitude kicked in, and sternly I said, "What's up dude?"

Friendly, he replied, "How you doing man? You kind of scared me. Coming from between those cars like that, I didn't see you, but excuse me. I guess I wasn't paying much attention."

More relaxed, but still on alert, I said, "That ain't nothing 'bout nothing. You kind of scared me too, and I live in this hood.

After sensing that this boy wasn't any kind of threat, I defused my defensive posture and readjusted my attitude. Even though the boy was white, there was still no need to feel confrontational. I inquired, "Are you lost?"

With a hint of confusion in his voice, he looked around and said, "Maybe so, and maybe not. I think that this railroad track will take me to Beach Street. That's where I live."

As a matter of verification, I said, "Good guess. You've got about a quarter of a mile to go, then you'll be there."

"Thanks," he said, and turned to continue his walk.

Since the boy seemed quite friendly, I decided to offer him some of my neighborhood's treasured sweet treats. Along various sections of the railroad tracks, grew some of nature's sweetest treats. Treats of wild berries, plums, peaches and an assortment of other goodies. Surely, I knew all of the choice fruit bearing spots. On many occasions, I'd eaten the fruit on my walk from school. It kept me from getting hungry before Mama made it home from work to prepare dinner. She worked across town, making furniture on some kind of an assembly line. Usually it was about five thirty in the evening before she could get started cooking. So, six o'clock was chow time. Neighborly, I shouted out, "Hold up, dude. If you got the time, I've got some good stuff that will help make your walk easier."

Curiously he said, "What kind of stuff you talkin 'bout?"

I pointed my finger, and as the boy's eyes followed, I said, "How about some of nature's best?"

"Wow!" He shouted, "I ain't never seen berries that big before, and plums too. Let's eat!"

While reaching out and picking some of the fruit, I boasted, "I can guarantee you that this is the best fruit in town. Make sure you try the figs before you go. And by the way, what's your name?"

He said, "I'm Jeff, good to meet you. What's your name?"

"I'm Jason, good to meet you too. You said you were going home, but where are you coming from?"

While still wiping fruit juice from his face and mouth, he said, "I go to White Settlement High. We had late band practice and I forgot to tell my mother to pick me up, then I missed the bus. That's when I decided to walk. I kind of figured this railroad track would be a good short cut."

"Sounds like a plan, Jeff. You're on the right track and going in the right direction. It was cool meeting you, but now, I've got to be going. I've got a game to play later today. So, you take care."

Jeff cleaned his berry-stained hands on his jeans, reached for his books, and said, "Okay man, you take care too. And thanks a lot for the fruit."

As he kneeled to gather his books from along the side of the railroad track, one fell from the stack and I couldn't help but notice how many he had. I inquired, "That seems to be a heavy load for such a long walk."

"It sure is. And I've got a lot of homework for some strict teachers. I'm in the tenth grade. What grade are you?"

"I'm in the tenth too, but we don't have books like those. What kind of subjects are you studying?"

He handed me the books one at a time, as he said, "This one is on social studies. "I've also got history, new math, and a music book. They give us too much homework."

Understandingly, I said, "I can sure see what you mean. Our school will only let us bring home one book at a time." Then it occurred to me that it was probably because we never had anything that difficult for homework anyway.

"Well," he said. "I've got too many books, and too much homework."

I was more than a little confused in discovering that this boy and I were on the same grade level. His books and study material seemed foreign to me. I hadn't been exposed to any of the material that he had. I continued to preview his books, as he scanned my one. Yet, while thumbing through my book, he seemed to look perplexed. Then he sputtered out, "I know this course. This is what we took last year. Look man, what a coincidence. This is even the same book I had."

Surprised and confused by his comment, I said, "Did you memorize the book that well, or what?"

Jeff quickly opened the book and pointed to its inside cover, then said, "Look right here at this list of names. My name is right there. See, Jeff Gregory. This is your name, isn't it?"

Reluctantly, I nodded and said, "Okay, that's my name, Jason Philips. But anyway, like I said before, its time for me to make it on in now. You be cool, and take it easy until next time."

Jeff waved good-bye, and replied, "Okay, man, you take it easy too. Maybe we'll see each other again."

As I tuned to walk away, I wasn't angry with Jeff, but as sure as the days are long, I was angry with somebody for something. My educational confidence had been disassembled and I was very much disappointed. Wasn't any wonder why I could ace every test that my school gave me, they were giving me old books. I was using that school system to take my best shot at preparing to succeed, and they had been giving me old news, second-hand supplies. To me, that was just as bad as going off to a war with blanks in your gun. I thought out loud, "The nerve of society. For them to take such a cheap shot, they ain't nothing but a bunch of jerks." I was totally ticked off.

Over the years, I'd developed a plan to do well in school. Mama, Reverend Clark, my teachers and many others had always told me that education held the keys to success, and I believed them. But now I figured that if I had to play the game of education with people who deal from the bottom of the deck, by the time that I could receive my keys to success, they might have changed the locks on the doors. Out in the street, in the midst of wolves, it was clearly understood that only the strong survives. Nobody prepared me for the deception, that I found to be real, in our school's education system. I had no idea that cheating crooks would be on both sides of the fence, regular society and the underworld too. It was a rude awakening for me to find that I was in a game where even the umpires had hidden agendas. And since I figured that neither of the two types of learning systems, institutional or street, were going to cut me a square deal, I concluded that I'd just combine the good from them both to gaining an edge, an advantage in life. If I could become astute in both of those systems of learning how to live, it would be like having a secret weapon, a trump card that could offer me the element of surprise.

Chapter Two

All of the way home, I was feeling a rage that had no explanation or direction, but I only allowed my new awareness to fuel my burning desire to succeed. And upon my arrival home, I sat quietly immersed in my thoughts, only to soon be disturbed. Entering the house, and slamming the door, my big sister Evelyn, shouted, "Get up boy! You sittin' there like you're lost in space."

Looking up at her from my chair, I said, "Don't you worry 'bout that, Miss Boss Lady. I can handle my business. Anyway, why are you so late?"

My funny looking sister turned and said, "Don't you worry 'bout my business, Grumpy. You just better get your cone-head up and help me clean this house before Mama gets home."

I do believe that old sister of mine had the sharpest tongue in the south. I should've known better than to try mixing words with her. She always had some sort of comeback for whatever I had to say. She was only a couple of years older than me, and maybe, a bit more advanced in the ways of life. Although, when things were all said and done, I did learn a lot about women from listening to her. But for all of the tea in China, I'd never let her know that I thought she was quite an attractive young lady. We had lost our father in an auto accident during our earlier childhood. Evelyn had inherited his coarse and wavy black hair, along with his deep chocolate hue. That inheritance only complemented the sleek feminine features and soft brown eyes that she'd received from Mama. Between the two of us, Evelyn and I, our relationship was as thick as a brick. And when push came to shove, she and I had each other's back well covered. Even though we occasionally squabbled, we loved each other very much. But after she had finished her wise cracking statements, in my most demanding style, I responded like the chief dictator in charge, and said, "Check this out, you old ugly thing. Let's cut the smart remarks and just get through with this house job. And when we finish, I'm gonna go play me some basketball, gotta go show my game on the court. I want you to tell Mama that I just might be late for dinner."

Sternly looking at me, she said, "Basketball! Boy, once you finish cleaning your part of this house, who cares if you even eat?"

It didn't take long for me to finish my daily chores. And as soon as I'd finished, I was off to the court. We had a first class basketball court and some really big time games were played on it. Some of the other kids from around the neighborhood, and me, had found some strong two-by-fours that made for a sturdy pole and a wide piece of smooth plywood for a solid backboard. We also had an authentic leather ball and a goal with a net that one of the fellows had gotten for his birthday. Our outdoor arena even had a name. We called it, The Dust Bowl. We called it that because we played on a dirt turf that was covered with loose gravel. And whenever we would get a good heated game of three-on-three going on, we would stir up a cloud of dust bigger than The Lone Ranger and his horse Silver could've kicked up.

When I arrived at the court a game was already in progress. Three new guys were dominating the games against Homer and his pals. The new guys kind of reminded me of King Kong, Mighty Joe Young and the Missing Link, just three big gorillas. But the team to beat was sitting under a tree at the court's sideline, my two homeboys, Jake and Zak, waiting for me to join them. I shouted, "Yo! You dust busters need a third player? Looks like it's about time to regain home court advantage on those three farmers."

Zak raised a clenched fist and shouted, "Perfect timing J.P., my main man!"

Jake gave up his high-five, and said, "Right on time, Long Shot J.P. Its time to send those three wanna-be players to another hood."

As my buddies and I exchanged greetings, I heard a voice come from the other side of the court. It was the voice of the fellow that looked like King Kong. He shouted, "Down! Later for them three ladies, we want some players. Give us another set of chumps!"

The defeated team of Homer and company eased off the court in a daze while the Missing Link, minus his three front teeth, looked to the sideline and flipped the soul finger to me and my home boys.

Jake shouted, "I got game! We be next!"

I never was really a big kid, but I could hold my ground on the basketball court. On our home court I was known as, Long Shot J.P., with moves to the basket as smooth as silk. Plus, for this game, I had an edge. Big Jake and brother Zak were on my side, and they both were as big and strong as oak trees. On the way to the court, I passed Homer and jokingly said, "Better luck next time buddy. Why don't you and the other rookies take a seat, and then take some notes? The boys and me gonna show y'all how to play some grown folks ball."

The ball goes out first to the winner. Kong threw the ball into play at mid-court, where Mighty Joe, wasting no time at all, went straight up for a jumper. The only problem with the shot, was Zak. It was as if he was in automatic hyper drive with rockets on his shoes. He leaped and rejected the shot clear across the court. In the heat of competition, he yelled at Mighty Joe, "Not today, buddy. This be my house, and you ain't puttin nothin in this hoop!"

With the ball out once again, I easily moved around the Link and showed them why I was referred to as, Long Shot. I took a fifteen-foot jumper and shouted as the ball dropped through the rim, "Swoosh! Nothing but net."

Our opponents became a little irritated, and quite physical. That game shaped up to be my kind of contest. In spite of the rough play, there was never a doubt that we were going to regain the neighborhood crown. Right at the onset, I received the inbound pass from Jake and passed it to Zak, who passed it back. I caught the ball on a dead run toward the basket. With a couple of behind-the-back dribbles, I left Mighty Joe in his tracks. My smooth moves had created an open lane to the basket large enough to be a runway at the airport. Kong was jockeying for position under the basket, making ready to reject my shot. Suddenly, in my mind his face was replaced by the face of that Gregory kid, the boy on the railroad tracks who showed me the true colors of our cheating educational system. Kong's massive body seemed to now represent a society that had to be altered from its position of imbalance, and I was going to be the one to do it. With faith and determination to go along with my talents, I felt that I could conquer any foe. I made a direct air attack on Kong, one on one, and skillfully used what was then called my famous double pump fake with a special yo-yo twist to set up my behind-the-rim monster dunk. Then my view was abruptly darkened. Out of nowhere, Kong's elbow came crashing down on my head. For me, it was lights out. I was in a cloud of dust with a halo of stars spinning around my head. But as the dust started to clear, and my composure began to return, the halo of stars grew dimmer. I began to have thoughts that sometimes it doesn't matter how good you are, circumstances can alter your winning moves. I was sitting on the ground thinking that nobody can win them all, when Jake's voice rang in my ear. Awakening my senses, he said, "You all right dude? You gonna be okay man?"

Before I could respond, Zak blurted out as he was shaking me, "Jason, get up man, you gonna be okay?"

Then I arose from that haze of dust and shouted, "Foul! That had to be a tech. I need time out. Get me a substitute in here, or something."

Slowly, I walked toward a tree near the sideline to sit and regroup my senses. Still in a daze, I realized that I had been knocked out. Probably, only for a few seconds, but still rendered unconscious. As I sat under the tree, the sky above me darkened from the shadows of Mighty Joe, the Link and Kong, they towered over me. Then I heard the Link say, "Good game little dude. We got to have a rematch."

Kong looked down at me and said, "Sorry about the elbow little brother. It might not make it feel no better, but you got a good game. And that bruise, its just part of the program. Anyway, we gotta go. Might get a chance to play you fellows again sometime."

I responded with a low-five slap from the three of them, and said, "Sure, ain't nothing but a thang. Good game guys, try again next time."

I came to the conclusion that those three competitors were halfway decent fellows after all. Their inquiring about my condition showed good sportsmanship. I think they used the games to vent frustrations. Those boys played a good game, and they could literally put your lights out. But on the real side, the best team had won. When I took that last shoot, they delivered a knockout punch, but we won the game. My yo-yo twist from behind the rim monster dunk had gone in. I had made the winning shot and it felt as good as a breath of fresh air. I could hardly believe that after getting totally knocked out, I was still able to take care of business. My mentality of always having the winning edge had begun to come back. With my reinforced attitude, nobody and nothing could've stopped me. I was ready for tomorrow. I was prepared for the good, bad or ugly in life and was comfortable in believing that I could always win. With a restored confidence, a large appetite for dinner and a slight headache from Kong's elbow, I arrived home to Evelyn's investigating mouth, yelling, "What in the world happened to you boy? You've got a knot on your head as big as a grapefruit. Mama! Come look at this boy's head."

Gently, I reached up and touched my forehead, and without a doubt, she was right; I did have a knot on it. Shortly afterward, Mama rushed into the room and gasped for breath, as she said, "Boy! What happened to you, are you okay?"

I was a little shaky, but I said, "I'm okay Ma. It ain't nothing but a war wound from the basketball game. Evelyn is just making noise over nothing."

Mama ushered me into the bathroom for first aid and Evelyn comforted, as she said, "You better be glad that I even care."

Seeing my wound in the mirror, more than justified my sister's concern. Fortunately for me, it looked worse than it felt. But Mama, still gently applied a cold compress to my injury as she also admonished, "Jason, you have got to be more careful. Every time I look around, you're bruising or hurting something on yourself. Don't make me have to worry about you boy. You're the only son I've got; you've got to start taking better care of yourself."

Mama did what mamas do, soothed me with cold compresses and tender love and care, as I said, "Don't worry about me Mama. You know I can take care of myself. Plus, the good news is that we won the game. But Ma can we please eat now? I'm 'bout to starve."

"Sure we can, son. It's good that you feel like eating. I guess I'll just have to understand that boys will be boys."

Greens, corn, chops, and hot water cornbread were just the prescription that I needed to help me forget about my throbbing pain. I could've also done without Evelyn's snickering and pointing her finger at my head all through dinner. Later that night, I went into Mama's room to see if she could explain the confusion that was going through my mind. I had restored my confidence from that awakening experience with Jeff Gregory by releasing my aggressions on the basketball court, but I didn't know how to deal with the scar that racial prejudice had suddenly imprinted in me. I felt like I'd been cheated, as Mama tried to explain and comfort me. She said, "Jason, in many ways you have been protected from racial prejudice, but problems between Black and White people do exist."

Arrogantly, I assured, "Hey, Mama, I know about white folk. They ain't 'bout to mess with me."

"Son, be quiet and listen. You're a fine boy and I believe that you could out talk any attorney, but now isn't the time for that. This is not your problem alone, it's worldwide, and you need to do your best to understand that. Unfortunately, America's majority, the decision makers of our society, used their power to set up a system that denies black people equal educational opportunities. They're trying to use it as a method of slowing down our progress. Realize this Jason, men and women of color are not always fairly judged on their own merit, or their individual character. Many of us are judged in stereotypical ways."

I was a little irritated and slightly confused, as I said, "That sounds like a crime to me."

Detecting my confusion and irritation, Mama continued to explain, "Son, God judges, that is not your job. Your father and I moved here from Arkansas to help reduce the bigotry that you and your sister might encounter. Both of us knew that moving to Memphis wouldn't exempt you two from it totally. However, this city has a history of black and white people being aware of each other and still giving one another enough respect and space to avoid confrontation. That's why we live secure in this town, even though bigotry is very much alive and well."

Curiously I said, "The way you put it, sounds like they stay on their side of town and we stay on ours. Is that the reason that I rarely see any white people?"

"Yes," she said. "That does have a lot to do with keeping the peace. But to ease your mind about your education as a black man, there are some things that you do need to know. An effort is being made by our leaders to make sure that you can get the same opportunity as anyone else. They want to desegregate the school system so that black and white people can go to school together and get the same education. Waymon is a very good school, but you know just as well as I, it is the exception to the rule when ranking other schools that our people attend. Be patient, it won't be long before you can go to White Settlement, or any of those other, so-called, good schools. I think that they are calling this new legislation, busing."

Perplexed, I said, "Busing. I'm not real sure that I like that idea Mama. Sounds to me like I'm gonna end up in a strange place, surrounded by strange people."

"That's probably true," she said. And in an attempt to find something positive to say about the legislative solution, she also added, "Just try to consider that you will be getting a better education, plus you won't have to walk to and from school anymore."

Suspiciously, I said, "Something 'bout this plan sounds close to being as bad as used books."

Mama smiled and gave me a tight hug, as she said, "Well, however the system goes, it's still the only solution for right now. I know that you already have a mind of your own and I'm proud of your awareness. Remember that every civil right enjoyed by black people today, started with the awareness of one individual. If you really apply yourself and learn the ways of this world, some things you may be able to change. Jason, you are the best of the best, God loves you and Mama does too. Now, it's time for bed."

"Thanks for talking with me Ma; I really do feel better. One day, I'll find a way to let the world know that black people don't have to accept nothing from nobody to survive, because we can make it on our own. Goodnight Mama."

I went to my room, but not without hearing the final words from Evelyn, the dragon lady, when I passed by her room. Still instigating, she said, "Goodnight egghead."

I accepted her smart mouth wise crack and said, "That's right, and a good night to your big mouth self too." Then I whispered, "Thanks for caring about me."

That night I went to bed counting my blessings. I was a lucky guy to have a mother and a sister that cared so much for me. I was proud of my

Mama and Evelyn too. I knew that I had inherited my tough, aggressive and sometimes arrogant behavior and short-tempered ways from my Dad. But I also knew from the dialogues with Mama that there was a seed of diplomacy that could've passed from her to me.

Chapter Three

I developed a new attitude towards school. My intentions began to literally focus towards trying to absorb all of the teachings I could. And as the school days came and went, I attacked each one of them like I was a dry sponge in a bucket of water. I did my schoolwork because I wanted to be well trained. But on the weekends, I also tried to have as much fun as possible. Most of those weekends I hung out with my number one buddy, Bert Crane. He always managed to find a way to help make my weekends interesting. Early one Saturday morning I answered a knock on my front door. It was Bert. He greeted me with an ear-to-ear smile. "What's happening J.P., my main man?"

"Ain't nothing going on. Tell me something good."

"Man, everything is everything. I've got some good news. My folks went to check up on my aunt, and they gonna be gone all day. We got plenty of weenies in the icebox, so let's do us a barbecue. What do ya' think 'bout that?"

With a delicious image of barbecued hot dogs tempting my taste buds, I said, "Now that sounds like a plan my man. But won't your parents get mad about you using their stuff?"

I stepped outside to keep our conversation from being overheard, as Bert said, "I can tell you ain't never barbecued before. Don't worry, homeboy, we ain't gonna mess up nothing. I got skills. We can cook the dogs on Dad's grill, outside, with no mess. All we gotta do is just empty out the old coals and it'll be a done deal. Dude, its hot dog time. Get with the program."

"Okay man. Hold on a minute while I go get my sneakers." In a matter of minutes we were on our way. Although, using my hindsight, I should've considered the source of the offer. Bert was my pal, but sometimes, he seemed to do things without giving them very much thought. He had gotten me into trouble on more than just a few occasions, but we always had tons of fun. He and I met when I was in the second grade. He was three years older than me, had a sandy red afro, and his complexion was about three shades darker than mine. Although he wasn't really a big fellow, he was bulky enough to intimidate a lot of the neighborhood kids. Both of us had adventurous, inquiring minds and we liked hanging out with each other. His parents were friends with Mama and Dad also, before Dad's accident. They'd visit each other and have house parties with card games and other adult social entertainment favorites like, dominos, etc. Although for us, our parents knowing each other was just more adult eyes to keep a check on Bert's and my attempts at getting into trouble. In those days, most of the adults in our community kind of helped other parents keep their kids on the straight and narrow road of doing right. Even though adults in the area communicated, old Bert and I managed to get into some childish misbehavior, anyway. Once, while spending the night at his place, we ran out of things to do. While we were thinking of ways to keep ourselves busy, he said, "I got a good idea J. Do you want to know what it is?"

Suspect, I replied, "Sure, I want to know what your light bulb is showing you."

Snickering and slapping his knee, he said, "You gonna like this, my man. I know where we can find some fireworks that look like sticks of dynamite. You take one of them bad little dudes, snap off the cap, strike the thing across the top of the tube and it'll start a torch like flame that we can launch into the air. Man, I'm telling you, the thing will come down with the blaze still going strong enough for another toss. It'll be just like launching Roman candles."

The thought of fireworks was tempting. The Fourth of July, New Years Eve and Labor Day were about the only times they were sold. However, I should've known that if Bert could get his hands on some, they would've had to been stolen. But the fireworks actually turned out to be railroad flares. Later that day, close to sunset, we took some flares from a caboose and made a get a way. Afterwards, we began to snap off flare caps, scratch tubes and throw the things like Roman candles being blasted from a cannon. I could see a glaze in Bert's eyes; he was fascinated with the intensely glowing and colorful flames being generated by the ingredients of our missiles. I figured my buddy had a little bit of a firebug in him, but we both had a great time with our fireworks exhibition. At that age, we were old enough to do wrong, but not smart enough to know that the railroad had their own special agent forces to protect and serve their company. Although we soon found out when their officers showed up on Bert's doorstep. Turned out that the caboose raid was my first, but not Bert's. The railroad agents had traced him from some of his solo episodes and were not aware of our escapade. Of course, Bert never mentioned my name. Ironically, the Rail Company wasn't concerned about the missing flares; they were concerned over the raids when Bert had tested the strength of some of the caboose's windows. He was busted for vandalism and his parents had to pay one hundred fifty dollars for the damages. My homeboy and I saw each other again, but it wasn't for a long time. He was put on a long lock down punishment.

Bert was a friend that I always felt I could trust, and as we arrived at his house on barbecue day, we were ready to have some fun. "Let's get ready to fire up the grill J. You can fill this thang with charcoal while I go get the dogs, buns and some lighter fluid to start us up a blaze."

When he returned I'd finished my charcoal assignment, so as he attended the food and fire, I decided that I'd share my Jeff Gregory encounter with him. I felt it was important to see if it mattered to him. I also wanted to again try exploring my own thoughts. I explained to him what had happened, but responding to me, he first cautioned, "Stand back brother. I need a little room to start this fire." Then he threw several matches on the fluid saturated briquettes, before elaborating on my experience. "That's a low down and dirty shame, that thang you talkin 'bout. But it all ain't nothing but a system, a game, and all we got to do is learn ways to beat it. What else is a man supposed to do? Anyway, right now my biggest problem is this stupid fire won't stay lit."

I was able to vent my frustrations, but I didn't like Bert's response. Yet alert, I cautiously waited for him to stop squirting fuel on the charcoals, and then said, "You really don't seem to care about school anyway. I've been telling you, you're gonna get cut short with that attitude. But right now, you need to be careful with that fire."

"Chill out man. I've seen my Dad do this a hundred times. But word up on that school business, don't you worry 'bout brother Crane getting cut short on nothing. The street is my game and that's all I need to know. I'm gonna get rich, right here in this hood."

"Yeah, well I know that you can handle your game, but if you don't get your diploma, you ain't gonna be too much of nothing. And I'm still saying that you really need to stop squirting that stuff all over the flames like that, airhead."

Ignoring my warning, but boasting and assuring, he said, "Ha! Diploma, don't make me laugh. I've got that thing under control better than I've got this fire.

"Now how in this world can you fix your mouth to say that? You're the same dude that has been in the eleventh grade for two years."

"Look man, I'm a little older than you are, so I've learned a few tricks that you don't know yet."

"Like what?"

"Like getting my diploma, man, that's what. Check this out. I done already failed eleventh grade two times, and that's the limit."

Suspiciously I said, "Sounds like you been sniffing that lighter fluid."

"Ha, ha. That's because you don't know what I know. The same system that you been ragging out, they got to pass me. This be the third time for me, and they got a special policy. It's called the three-timer rule. It helps to keep the school from looking bad."

With a blank expression, I said, "You're gonna have to break that one down for me. That don't make no sense at all."

As he turned over the hot dogs, he explained, "Simple, bean-brain. A student who fails twice is automatically promoted to the next grade. You see if they try keeping somebody in the same grade forever, it makes everybody look bad, even them folks downtown. Make any sense to you now?"

Before I could respond to Brother Crane's logical explanation of nonsense, he suddenly shouted, "Wow! Get back, man! We got too big of a blaze going up in here!"

As he shouted and I stood in confusion, bright colored flames began to bellow from the grill and a haze of smoke engulfed the both of us. Immediately, Bert began to beat at the flames, until he knocked the grill over. The heated charcoals and flames spread along the paved driveway's path and on to the grass. Now, nervously he stammered, "What we gonna do J.? Do something man!"

I joined in and stomped at the flames, also to no avail. "I don't know what to do Crane, I ain't no fireman!"

Then Bert rushed behind the garage and came back with one of his usual patterns of ideal thinking, solving a problem while creating another. Running from behind the garage with a bucket of water, he doused the flames and shouted, "I got it buddy, get back!"

He may have thought he had things under control, but what we witnessed was one weird spectacle. And in disgust, I said, "Ahea man! Look at that. What in the world have you done?"

For a moment, we both just stood and watched the mess. Then Bert said, "I didn't know that was my Dad's bucket of fishing minnows. He's gonna break my neck. Man, I thought it was a bucket of plain old water."

The driveway was covered with heated charcoals and dirty weenies, along with grassy buns and flopping scorched minnows. After a brief assessment of our situation, I looked at my partner in crime, and said, "What are we gonna do now, since we can't eat?"

Bert briefly surveyed the area for damage, then said, "No harm, no foul. We can hose this mess clean in no time at all; throw away the burnt dogs and them little fish. Man, won't nobody be the wiser. But since we can't eat, and I can't replace the stinking minnows, it all sounds like wine time to me. I need a drink. How 'bout you?

"It sure sounds a lot better than minnows and hot dogs. Let's go get us a bottle?"

"Right on brother J."

Chapter Four

Bert and I did our, clean up to cover up task at his house, then we went to our favorite bottle shop. Buck George's liquor store was the main spot for us to hangout. There was a store next to it that sold greasy hamburgers. One of those burgers with onions would kill the scent of a goat's butt; they were my insurance policy to keep wine odors from being detected on my breath by Mama. Surely, this was one aspect of my life that she knew nothing about. But to be honest, I really never liked drinking anyway. I didn't like the taste of it, smell of it nor the stupid way that it made me feel. I only drank it because I wanted to look cool in the eyes of the other guys. Actually, most of the time I only faked drinking. Little did the others know, but what went into my mouth when I turned the bottle up, most of it went back into the bottle when it came back down. Thanks to the brown paper bag that we used to hide the bottle, nobody was able to detect me faking it. Although the little that did get into my system, still made me feel stupid.

We hit the corner and gave up our high-five dap to all of the brothers that were standing around. Then we began to joke, jive and drink with them on the lot behind the liquor store. We were a diverse group, but one of the bunch was considered to be dangerous. That boy's name was Archibald Benson, a.k.a. T-Roll. That crazy bonehead boy carried a hatchet stuffed in the back pocket of his pants, and he was not beyond using it, but he could be reasoned with. I never considered him to be a very sharp thinker. Usually, his brain seemed to be kept in the same place as his hatchet. Really, I didn't like him very much and I think he liked me even less. While one group of our bunch socialized, another group of fellows was shooting dice. T-Roll was in the dice game. He eyed my presence on the scene, rolled the dice against the liquor store's wall and talked jive, "Ain't no shame in my game. I'm a winning machine, taking everybody's green cash."

For reasons unknown to me, on that boy's next roll, he decided to put me to a test. He rolled a seven on the dice and shouted out, "Ouch! Make me wanna holler, just like JP's mama. Fade me and pay me, suckers."

T-Roll had pushed the wrong button, turning on my immature and unrestrained temper. When he made another roll of the dice, snake eyes changed his luck. Smirking, he looked over his shoulder at me, and said, "Guess I shot one time too many. But for you, punk, and all these other losers, I'll still roll one time for the road. Gimme a seven, dice."

Why me, I'll never know, but he had come to the right place to pick a fight. He stooped over for his next roll and I tried to lose one of my sneakers up his butt crack. I kicked the hatchet right out of his back pocket. And to keep things even, Bert reached down and grabbed it so it wouldn't be used to stop me from settin that bum, T-Roll, straight on how to show respect. I broke that boy down and began to bounce rapid lefts and rights off the side of his head like it was a punching bag. There was no way under the sun that I was going to let my reputation be marred to the degree that he was trying to. Then as fellow brothers began to separate the two of us, I dotted his behind with a few electric leg-jacking kicks, while delivering my parting message. "You better learn some respect! You can act a fool as much as you like, but you better show respect when you're talking 'bout a lady. Especially, when she is my Mama!"

After the fight was broken up, I didn't feel much like drinking any more. So I turned to my buddy and said, "Yo, Brother Bert, I'm gonna catch you later. Think I'll go home."

He seemed to understand and said, "Okay, I guess you might be a little tired after all of that exercise. I'm gonna put this news on the pipeline so the underworld will know how you kicked the boxing out of that clown. You grew up a little bit today, partner. Plus, this news will help keep some of the other young punks from trying to test you."

I said, "Thanks man." Although inside of me, I wasn't too proud of having to fight with a brother, even though he was a nut bucket. As I was walking home, I couldn't help but to realize the rage that existed deep inside of me, fueling my already quick temper. This was surely something that I would have to find a way to get under control. But suddenly my train of thought was interrupted by a friend and respected neighbor. He yelled and waved his hands to get my attention, calling, "Come over here, boy."

"What's up Charley? What can I do for you?"

Loudly, he scolded, "You can bring your wild butt over here, just like I told you to start with. This old man needs to tell you something."

I walked across the street to his porch and said, "What's up?"

"What's up?" He roared, "Who do you think you are. Do you think you're Muhammad Ali, Joe Louis, Smoking Joe Frasier or who? Why you be out in them streets fighting and acting like you ain't got good sense."

I mumbled and shuffled as I said, "Man, is this a gossip town or what? The sweat from the rumble ain't dried on me yet and you know about it already."

Charley yelled, "That ain't the point, knot-head!"

In an adolescent disgust for people that gossip, I said, "Any way, I know that's a shame. Folks just need to mind their own business."

Stern and disciplinary, he admonished, "You been carrying on like a wild animal. You just be lucky your Mama don't know about the grapevine news on the streets. Now, what'cha gonna do, kick my butt for talking 'bout your Mama too?"

"Ahea, come on Charley, you know it ain't like that."

"You've got that shipment right. I know a lot. I know that you need to sit your butt down and let me school you on some facts about life, little brother."

Calmly I took a seat at a card table across from Charley on his porch. Mr. Charles S. Flag was not considered to be a busy body. He was a respected elder and highly recognized by everybody in the hood. He was well thought of by all, in spite of the fact that he drank alcohol like a fish does water. The Flag Man had the same kind of wisdom as described by the poet Langston Hughes when he wrote his works about the man named, Simple. I looked at Charley, and said, "Okay, Mr. Flag I'm listening."

"Jason, I know you ain't no fool. Why don't you tell me what the real problem is? That crazy boy Bert didn't talk you into fighting, did he?"

"No, that's not it. Bert and me, we cool."

"He is cool; a cool fool is what he is."

"Well, that may be true, but I do believe that I can trust him."

Charley pondered my comment, then said, "It's thangs 'bout that boy you don't know. I've seen his kind before, but I can also understand your thought. He probably can be a best friend, and some people's worst nightmare. But let's stick with you Jason. What is wrong Son?"

I opened my thoughts to Charley, revealing my loss of trust in the school system and how that punk, T-Roll, had simply pushed the wrong button at the wrong time. I admitted to him how that boy had only been a target for me to unload my frustrations upon. He listened, and then took another sip of bourbon before giving me his wisdom. "Boy, you gonna be all right. Let me share a little bit of something with you that folks ain't been saying out loud. Education is important. However, it's also lopsided toward those that are in control. The people who are in power don't want you to have nothing that will let you learn how to get out of their oppressive grasp. So you just remember that when you play with the card sharks of society, they are likely to deal from the bottom of the deck. That's why the street-wise brother has learned to always palm his trump hold card. The experienced player only throws down his trump, when it's least expected. Learn the rules of the game Jason, and how your opponent plays. That's how you calculate your next move."

I wasn't sure if Charley was giving me advice, or scolding me, but as my friend lowered his brown bag covered liquid lunch from his lips, in an ignorant and arrogant tone, I said, "Why you be telling me what's what in life? I'm young, but I ain't no rookie. I can handle myself. What's the moral to this rap anyway?

Calmly he said, "Listen boy. I'm not gonna get upset with you 'cause I know how bad you need help, but don't you be getting impatient with me. You just ain't gettin the message. I know you don't understand all that I'm trying to say, but just get as much of it as you can. These are some cold-blooded facts, and you will have to understand them sooner or later, or be lost. Black men can't get help from any group that controls any amount of power to act in their favor. But together, we can create our own controlling power of favor. And this can never be achieved with us fighting each other. Fighting is for the ignorant and will lead directly to killing. Now you tell me, who's gonna stop a black man from killing another one? Nobody! Folks will just let him die."

I kind of shuffled my feet, as I said, "Come on now Charley, don't nag at me 'bout fighting again. I don't need help from those kinds of people anyway."

Shaking his head in side-to-side motions, he said, "You don't know what you need, and if you don't understand how this game of life is being played, you will end up taking help in any form that it comes in. Do you really think somebody that has already made a mark in society will bail your poor black self out of poverty? Well, think again, buddy. Even help from the select sophisticated elite of our own black people cannot be expected, mostly because they only give to pacify their own guilt complexes. They never give anyone enough assistance to do as well as they are. It's unfortunate, but our people are beginning to demonstrate an attitude of I've got mine, now you go and get yours. It's a selfish yet bitter truth. But Jason, your role in life is to find a spirit-filled peace in a unity of sharing what has been put on this earth for us all to enjoy. You have to be one of our leaders of hope for it to become a fact. Prepare yourself, so that you will be able to cut new ground on your road to success."

I paid close attention as that gentlemanly street scholar articulated his assessment of our people. He continued to teach, "You take these words little brother. All throughout this country's history, or since we came over in them boats, ships or whatever you wanna call them, our regal people have been kicked in the butt. Many of us have even been taught to act like they like it. You don't know our people's history. I hope that will start to change after today. Learn our people's history in order for you to learn about yourself. Don't allow others to dictate your future because you are the man for the future. Now promise me, no more fighting with your brothers."

I shook his hand and promised, "Thanks Charley, I do need to check my priorities. I'm gonna let your information sink into my head. Thanks again, and please excuse my behavior. You take care Sir." He bid me farewell with a smile, and another sip of his bourbon juice.

Chapter Five

Overall, I was a pretty good kid, in spite of me not letting Mama know of all the little things that I might have gotten into. I had a great love and respect for her, but I never feared her. She never believed in physical punishment, only guidance based on her trust in me. And, I never wanted her trust in me to be broken. The mere thought of doing something to hurt her, or cause myself to be an embarrassment, brought a mental anguish to me that was enough discipline to keep my sights mainly focused on what I believed was right. That's why whenever my curiosity of life did carry me into the realms that I thought might disappoint her; I'd at least try to not get caught. I understood that it hurts to hurt someone that you love. So, I was really relieved when a week had gone by and I hadn't heard anything from her about me fighting. It was a safe bet that the word of my actions hadn't gotten to her. I was also happy that Mom hadn't found out about my escapade because we had a family outing planned that week, and I surely didn't want our trip to be spoiled because of her being upset with me. Family outings were rare for us to manage, but that weekend Mama was taking us to the zoo. When we finally arrived at the gates of the City Park, I knew for sure that Mama would never find out about the fight. I really felt that I'd gotten away with something, and since I'd beat up that chump, I wasn't scared of nothing. I knew that from then on, wherever I'd go on the streets of our neighborhood, those corner hood-rats were gonna respect me. And Mom didn't have to know nothing about that.

As we started walking through the grounds of the park, Evelyn, acting all mature and culturally refined, looked to Ma and suggested, "Can we walk through the botanical gardens first? I'd like to smell the fresh flowers, before we visit Jason's monkey friends."

Mama smiled, but then warned, "Don't start trouble with your brother. Up until now, both of you have been very cooperative on this trip, and I intend for it to stay like that. Act like this is family day. We can't make them often, but we can make them happy and memorable."

I agreed with her, and said, "Ain't no problem Mama. I know she ain't doing nothing but teasing. Don't make no difference what she says anyway. I know she loves me."

My sister looked at me, smiled and kind of rolled her eyes. Mama gave us both a hug and started leading us towards the gardens. As we passed an intersection, a four way sign read with directional arrows pointing, north to see the botanical garden, south for the cats of the wild, east for concessions, and west to see the elephants. Discreetly excited, I said, "Mama, if it's okay with you, I'll go see some of the animals. I can meet you and Evelyn in a little while. The zoo is for seeing animals, and I don't really want to see no flowers."

Mama allowed me to venture out on my own, but I walked away from my family on a mission. For me, unknown to the rest of my family, I had some unfinished business. I couldn't wait to face off with a big tired looking gray elephant. During our family's last outing to the zoo, that old bull had chumped me out. He had stood as still as a statue for the whole time that we were there. He didn't entertain me at all. It was kind of like he didn't even recognize my presence. I was determined to show that titan of an animal who was boss. I wanted that fat elephant to understand that I didn't come all of the way downtown and spend good money just to see him stand around doing nothing. Eating, swatting flies and fleas wasn't gonna be good enough. Fat boy was gonna dance today, or do something.

As soon as I got out of Mama's sight, I ran to the elephant's fenced island habitat and gathered a pile of good throwing rocks. Before anyone could see me, I fired the rocks at that bull as fast as possible. He only eyed me, maintained his stone-faced stance, then started to enjoy sucking down the popcorn I was using to lure him towards my direction. The bull also had luck on his side, Mama and Evelyn joined me sooner than expected, but I was too smart and too fast to get caught. So when they were not looking in my direction, I'd launch a barrage of rocks at the animal with lightening speed. It didn't seem to make much difference to the creature, lazily he continued to stand, stare, and eat my popcorn. Yet, good things always come to those who wait. Mama and Evelyn turned their heads to watch a flock of peacocks. And for me, that's when the fun began. When they turned away, I cranked up for a pitch that the great Hank Aaron couldn't have hit, a haymaker pitch that would've knocked fire out of that bull's ears. Turned out that the timing for my power pitch was more accurate for the elephant than for me, and probably more fun also. To my surprise, and right in the middle of my throw, came an unknown force. That brute of a creature raised his long trunk, and sprayed me with water that had the force of a fire hydrant. He hit me right in the face, in between the eyes with a blast that almost took my breath away. Although in the midst of the confusion, I did find wisdom. After all, I had gotten what I came for, a reaction from that chump. So, with no real reason to stay, I kicked up dust at a frantic pace, with my body in high gear, I was running scared. Mama screamed, "Stop boy! You're gonna run into something! Somebody please, help me catch him!" And to her rescue came Dudley, the do right zoo's security officer. He had been watching me all along.

I ran and I ran fast, until I spotted a safe haven, the zoo's indoor aquarium. I neared the building's entrance in full stride and was prepared to jump a bedding of hedges that was standing between me and the door, only to be slowed by a hand on my right shoulder, accompanied by the sound of the officer's voice, "Slow down little man. It's time to go back to your Mama."

Now there I was, the sly and cunning J.P., cold busted by the law. After being nabbed by that zoo cop, I realized that my crude prank had turned and the joke was now on me. As the officer escorted me, I found it a little hard to stay cool, because it was a little embarrassing. But also as he and I walked, I began to notice a distinct sound that was different from any of the regular zoo animal's sounds. Although the mystery of the sound's origin soon revealed itself as we neared my family. My old ugly sister was slapping her knees and laughing loud enough to start every dog in a radius of three neighborhoods barking. When we came closer to her, she began pointing her finger at me, heckling as she laughed louder than ever. But to add insult to injury, she began to take Polaroid snapshots of Mr. Cool being humbled. Mama, she just stood and watched, with a slightly restrained grin on her face.

Later that night I went into Mama's room as she lay in bed watching a television program. I said, "Mama, I need to talk to you. There seems to be too many things that I can't figure out."

She turned off the television and said, "All children are confused, and it's all a part of growing up. Come over here and sit. Between you and me, we can get you back on track."

I went over and sat next to her, and said, "I hope so, things just don't seem to be going like they're supposed to. I thought that I was kind of tough, but that elephant scared the fire out of me."

She smiled and said, "It wasn't that bad. You may have overreacted a bit, but don't try acting like you're super human. None of us are perfect Son, and I don't want you to think that you can be perfect in any way that you choose to be. Life ain't always nice; sometimes it's only an experience of trial and error. Don't you make things harder for yourself by growing up too fast. Enjoy living and enjoy being a teenager because there are many things that you'll have to make ready for. So, let's just take things a little bit at a time. And, I know a very good place to start. Why were you on the street corner fighting?"

With my eyes opened wide from the surprise, I said, "Ump. How'd you find out 'bout that?"

"That doesn't matter. All that really matters is for you to remember that you are a child, not slick, nor tough, just a child doing his best to become a good adult. Understand me Son; doing wrong is never a well-kept secret."

Humbly I looked into her eyes and said, "I'm sorry about the fight and for not talking to you about it. But you understand things Ma. I'm just trying to do the right things so that I can know how to make good decisions."

Mama's wisdom comforted me as she said, "I do understand things Jason, and I encourage you to stand up for what you honestly feel is right in your heart. You'll benefit from good judgment, but you'll still be responsible for your mistakes. Although, if you'd really like to make an assessment of your decisions, just take a look in the mirror and decide if you like the person that you see."

I leaned over, gave her a kiss on the cheek, and said. "I'll always remember that Mama. I love you."

"I love you too. Goodnight young man."

After that night I quit thinking that I was tough, and cunningly slick. I'd been made aware of how little I really did know. And thanks to Mama, I did understand that truth would always ring loudest in my heart. She made me feel that I was back on track and could overcome any injustices, even if some of my resources were being issued out in a long-handled spoon. But the one thing that I was most certain of, I would surely have to make a lot of appearances in front of my mirror.

I decided to change my attitude by centering it on the things that I felt would best feed my appetite for improvement. Street life had always been real, and in that lifestyle, I knew nothing came sugar coated. Fortunately, I'd already gained a lot of knowledge that would be useful throughout my life in that arena. So, I turned my concerns toward what was offered to me from our society's institutional learning. I believed that this was the area of knowledge where I'd been shortchanged, and succeeding in it became my focal point. Achieving an education from a higher learning institution was going to be my plan of finding out how the real players play in this game of life. Although to make a serious effort at achieving such a goal, I had to see less of my friend Bert, and my other homeboys. But most of all, I had to stop spending time with those punk thugs that hung out around the liquor store's lot. Still, I did miss hanging with my partners and the liquor store crowd. My isolation from them gave me the solitude that I needed to devote myself to my studies. My dedication to studying gave me a solid foundation to build my understanding of many things. And by the end of the year, all of my hard work paid off. I was tested, evaluated, interviewed and advanced up a grade. Suddenly, I was a senior.

Chapter Six

I was thankful for the people and the institution that had nurtured my growth. For me, learning had become a pleasure. My aggressive nature was rejuvenated in an understanding that knowledge was endless. I was also thankful for the caring, devoted and well-learned individuals who had guided me throughout my last year of school to become one of E. K. Waymon High's honor graduates. I wasn't the valedictorian, but I did get a scholarship. In addition, I also received an award for serving as captain of the debate team and was asked to speak on their behalf at our graduation ceremony. Mama was very proud of my achievements, but the two of us were most proud of Evelyn. During that same year, she'd gotten married. She and her husband, Daniel, moved to France. He was a career military man and that's where he was stationed. We missed her a lot, but she was happy and we were happy for her. Although, she couldn't attend my graduation, my special sister made sure that I'd always remember her. For graduation, she sent me a gold signet ring and a card that reflected her love and best wishes for me. It was good to know that distance hadn't affected our relationship. But distance wasn't the only reason for her not showing up for my graduation, she was also pregnant. I shouted three cheers for our family's expected edition, and Mama cried and said, "Thank you Jesus."

Being asked to speak and receive a prestigious award at our school was no joke to me. I wanted to express myself so that I could clearly represent a spirit of liberation through a good education. When I was preparing my speech, I was inspired to research and find out exactly what kind of person our school had been named after. Out of mere assumption, I'd always thought that E. K. Waymon was probably some elderly gentleman that, at some point in time, may have made a considerable financial contribution to the institution. But it turned out that Waymon was a much more worthy person than I'd given credit. "Mrs. Waymon was a Julliard honor graduate that had returned to help her old school in the hood. The renowned poet, songstress, composer, and concert pianist was the first person to shout to the world in song, "To be Young Gifted and Black." E. K. Waymon had been named after the artist known as, The High Priestess of Soul. The effect on me from discovering that piece of information was, a proud matter of fact. Graduation day came and patiently my fellow classmates and I sat in chairs on the floor of the school's crowed activity center, excited and anxiously awaiting the start of our ceremony. I spotted my good buddy, Homer. He waved and shouted from seven rows back, "It's on, it's on, and it's right on! Yo, yo, brother J., the party be at Dollar Bill's place. He's throwing a free set for us graduates at The Hole in the Wall. We gonna get down, down, down to the ground."

Gleefully I shouted right back, "I'm right on with the right on, brother, and ready to party down."

Along with a short, yet animated dance, Homer returned my shout. "I'm ready to get my groove on. You just remember to keep your speech short."

I smiled, and with an upward outstretched clenched fist of brotherly togetherness, I saluted my brother. Through the years Homer had been a great friend to me. He was a team player and always willing to help. Homer was truly one of those type people that you could always count on. He was a man of his word. But still, nobody wanted his non-playing self on their basketball team. That boy never had any skills on the court, but he could surely tell a great joke. There were times when he really believed that he was a comedian, a.k.a., Happy Homer, a real people-pleasing guy. Seeing him in the midst of my peers made me feel like I was about to close old beginnings, only to reach out towards the start of new endings.

Finally, I settled down to cherish the moment, and to finish listening to our guest speaker. It seemed as if he was going to talk forever. It was party time and I felt like he had already talked the sun down. But actually, he really was a very honest, sincere and knowledgeable person, whose introduction of me to the audience was extremely complimentary. He was so complimentary of me that by the time he had finished; I wanted to give brother man speaker a low-five slap dap greeting. But, since I didn't really think that he was cool like that, I approached our guest and respectfully shook his hand. After accepting the trophy, humbly I made my way to the podium and began my oration.

"Dear honored guest, distinguished alumni, family and friends; I would like to thank you for sharing this event with us. This is E. K. Waymon High's graduation ceremony. On behalf of our nationally acclaimed debate team, proudly, I accept this award." Then I lifted it into the air, blew the crowd a kiss, and continued. "Ladies and gentlemen, from all of us on this stage, we'd like for you to know that this day is a landmark in all of our futures for a brighter tomorrow. Today we're high school graduates, and in some form of our own choosing, all of us are looking forward to continuing our education. So, on behalf of my coeds and me, I'd like to thank E. K. Waymon High's faculty and the entire staff for assisting in our progressive developmental growth. You all have had a hand in making it easier for us to learn, by making us feel that you cared. Thank you for giving us a sense of being wanted, and a feeling of being at home. As a recipient of one of the honor awards that has been given today, I'd like to use this platform to express my feelings, some of my views about life and being a success at it. In order for me to draw my conclusions on this matter, I had to first answer a question that had once confused me. The question was what are the real standards by which our society measures success? I'd heard of and read about many men and women, from all walks of life who have been referred to as successful. Many of them are considered successful by their financial gains, others for their athletic ability, some for exhibiting a creative uniqueness, and a great many more for many material-related reasons. So, when I considered those standards of measuring as being our society's, only real measurements, I wonder why I've never heard of the word success being associated with anyone for just, simply being a good person. It's from those thoughts that I drew my own conclusion on what my measure of success would be. I believe in the words that I once heard come from the mouth of Reverend, Doctor Martin Luther King Jr., "The mind is the standard of a man." And, in me holding that philosophy as truth, success must be measured by a person's own standards and defined from within their heart's spiritual awareness.

Also, and most important, I'd like to express my wish for all of us on this stage, to never let our strides to achieving our goals, ever override our pride in our people's heritage of togetherness. From my limited knowledge, our American history has clearly shown me that since we've been on this soil, we've always been our own best source of life. And, that we all survive because of what we've done for each other over the years. America's history also dictates that black people will continue to progressively survive, but only if this pattern remains stable. That's why I'd like us all to understand the importance of our unity. That's also why I'd like us to understand that the newly proposed issue of busing will soon divide the black students of the future. Soon, only a few will have the advantage we've had in being educated by those that understand us best. With us being a part of the last of this segregated, but united system that we've been educated in, let us all try sharing the fellowship that we've experienced, with those that will soon face being strangers in strange places. Lets each of us pledge to become active, lifetime members, among the ranks of our prestigious alumni. This is one way we can help ensure that the predictions that our race of people will self-destruct, remains a myth. I would like for us all to realize that no matter which direction each of us goes in, our love can always lead us to peaceful and prosperous conclusions."

I finished my speech and left the podium with butterflies in my stomach, hoping that my bittersweet message had at least touched one. Yet as the audience applauded, I scanned the crowd and spotted Mama, with tear filled eyes. But me, I wasn't about to cry, even though I kind of wanted to. In our society, the human male species is a strange breed of animal that tends to consider the showing of emotions as a display of weakness. This trend of thinking has proven to be a behavior that has robbed men of a most effective way of venting all kinds of frustrations. Worst than that, this insane mindset has impeded our ability to fully enjoy and share in many a cherished moments. But still today, our society teaches men to suppress their feelings, even though we can't stop the emotion to cry from being felt. Men of this new macho-man era seem to have forgotten that, even Jesus wept. So, when I finished my speech and walked off the stage to a warm acceptance, overcome by the accolades, I fooled them all. I cried tears of joy on the inside. But on the outside, I only smiled.

At the end of the program, I stripped from my formal ceremony cap and gown, buttoned the vest on my three-piece tailor made suit, and headed for the nearest exit to catch up with my party bunch. But as I stepped outside, I looked up toward our school's flag. It was just blowing in the breeze, proudly displaying its red, black, and green hues, while mysteriously flying at half-mast. Since no one that I knew of had died, and this was supposed to be a day of new beginnings, the flag's position signified nothing that I could relate to. Although from the empty feeling that I had embedded in my soul, it may have been an omen telling me that the end of an era was near. Once I asked our guidance counselor what the colors of the banner meant, and she mild-mannerly responded, "At some point in your life these colors will reveal their meanings to you. It will be at some stage of liberation, a test to be figured out at a later date. But when you are made aware, and it will be at a time of liberation, there will be an alumnus waiting to assist you in your venture."

I didn't understand her answer, but to me, that flag warranted the same respect as the prestigious school it represented. Etched into my mind, it was to become a lasting visual memory of a fine institution.

CHAPTER SEVEN

Homer yelled to me from across the parking lot, "We got Mack's Mama's car, come on and ride with us."

I waved my hand and was about to reply when another car's horn blew. Suddenly, I had an unexpected smile on my face that stretched from ear to ear. A familiar voice from the queen of the nightlife scene, Madame Lucky, was gently calling out to me, "How about taking a ride with an old friend?"

"You can bet on that, I would love to ride with you, old friend." Immediately I turned and shouted out to Homer, "Y'all go ahead man, I'm gonna ride with Lucky. See y'all at the party." Then I swaggered over to Lucky's car, as she comfortably sat behind the wheel of her luxury automobile. It was a stylish, powder blue Brougham convertible sedan, with it's ragtop pulled back to expose a plush leather interior. The mobile was complete, with all of the bells, chimes, whistles, and it shined like newly minted money. I said, "What a pleasant surprise. You're still looking good, like a million and a half bucks, sitting in your dream machine."

Gracing me with a cute wink, she said, "Okay, I see you haven't forgotten that flattery will get you anything. Come on graduate; roll with me for a while."

I got into that automobile and sank into its soft leather seat, ready for a smooth ride. Slowly we pulled away from the parking lot and began to cruise down the street. "How have you been Lucky?

With a smile that displayed teeth that were as white as pearls, she said, "Things have been great, Jason. I've been taking care of business as usual, but the news came across the wire about you speaking at the ceremony. Surely, I didn't want to miss that for anything."

"Thanks, I'm glad that you were there. I hope I didn't bore everybody."

"Why you were great, just as I expected. All of your friends in the mix are proud of you too. You know, the better you do, the more it disproves the garbage that's being said about our people. Saying stuff like our people in the hood ain't got any hope. You the man Jason."

Every heavily populated metropolitan city in the USA has an organized group of individuals that control the operations of the major illegal money making activities that take place in their area. Things like gambling, prostitution, white-collar accounting scams money-laundering operations, drug peddling, auto chop shop rackets and a host of other avenues that lead to accruing large sums of money. Memphis wasn't exempt from it either. The exception to the rule was that our city had a likeness of that type of organization formed among Black people. I don't know what the White sector of town called their group; it may have just been called politics in general. But in the hood, we called our organization of underworld moneymakers, the mix. If there was any news worth hearing, or any money worth mentioning, it was controlled through the members of the mix. Lucky was a key member in the workings of the mix. Madame Lucky was a very attractive, robust, worldly lady who might have been in her mid thirties. She looked very well, but everything about her style of dressing seemed to scream, streetwalker. Yet, over the years, I learned a lot from her. She'd taken it as an obligation to teach me the ropes; an act of kindness that she felt would help keep a young brother from being uninformed about the ways of street life. When I would decide to hang out, she'd steer me to places where I could enjoy myself without getting into trouble, or killed. It was a well-known fact from within the circle of the underground that she was a sponsor on my behalf. She showed me how important it was to know that respected and influential people are in all walks of life. Some are from mainstream society, and some are not. But Lucky was one of the prime suppliers of special substances to the patrons of the track. The track was the name of our city's blue light district. It was a stretch of several streets that accommodated most of the underground activities. It was also, an area where many came to party and hang out. I learned at an early age that I wasn't a judge, neither a juror, accuser, nor executioner, so I didn't believe in putting labels on people for the choices they make in order for them to survive, because I haven't walked in their shoes. Lucky was a friend of mine and that was all I needed to know about her. While turning the radio volume up to the sounds of a solid rhythm and blues tune, she flashed her starlight smile and said, "We're gonna take a cruise around the track a few times, that will give me a chance to show you off while you're still in town."

With a perplexed look on my face, I said, "You know 'bout me leaving?"

"J.P., he be, a going off to Al-a-ba-ma. Going off to the u-ni-ver-si-ty."

"Well I guess you do have the dip on what's happening with me."

She assured me, "Don't worry about information that comes through the mix. In the organization, we're all behind you. Just because you buried your head, like an ostrich, in what you've been doing, that doesn't mean your friends ain't been checking up on what's been happening with you. Some of us know how important it is to help keep up with a young brother that's trying to do right."

"I appreciate the good looking out that all y'all do for me, Lucky. Don't think that just because I'm not around means that I've forgotten everybody, I ain't got nothing but love for all of y'all. But I had to get off to myself and learn dedication and discipline; you know what I mean."

She took my hand and squeezed it, as she said, "You were a baby when most of us started making money from the streets, but you're an original. We're gonna always be around for you, and your buddy, Bert. He's already training to run some things."

I looked at her with no sign of surprise, and said, "Considering that I already know him, I won't even bother asking what he might be involved in. Dude always has said that his expertise was taking care of business from some where within the mix. Personally, I think he can handle it."

"I think you're right," she said. "Give that boy another six months and he'll be a real contender."

As we rolled down the road, Lucky would periodically stop to check on her staff of distributors. She ran a well-oiled machine, a corporate culture with money flowing as smooth as silk. Without a doubt, she was an entrepreneur. After finishing her operation control inspection check, she suggested, "I'm getting thirsty. Let's roll up to the Rib Shack and have a root beer while I take a break."

"Good idea." I said, "I'm thirsty too, but a root beer, that ain't the best we can do. This is my graduation celebration."

She looked at me with a, don't try conning me, expression on her face, and said, "You can't play games with me, I know you don't like alcohol."

I gave a gasp of surprise, but she was as right as rain. I replied, "I'm glad you're my friend. I've always been able to be my real self when I'm with you. That's a comfortable feeling, and I like it. But a good friend can also tell when something is troubling his homey. I've noticed some-thing on your mind. Do you want to talk about it?"

Before she was able to reply, our curbside waitress had arrived, and politely asked, "What can I get for y'all?"

The Rib Shack was an innovative establishment for its day in time. It was a nice cafe styled restaurant that gave special attention to the serv-icing of its customers. You could just drive up to that joint, park, turn your lights on and they would come out and serve you, right in your car. And sitting in Lucky's plush convertible, on that warm day in May, there wasn't a restaurant in town with a better atmosphere. She turned to the waitress, and said, "Two root beers, please."

The waitress politely responded and left. Lucky looked at me through a set of serious eyes, and said, "You were right about something being on my mind, we do need to talk." After the waitress returned and served our beers, Lucky continued to share her concerns. She said; "This town is about to change, Jason. Things won't be the same, not much longer. The unity among black people is about to take a turn for the worst."

"Excuse me." I said, "I'm not quite following you, Lucky. I don't understand."

"You understand more than you are aware of, J. You feel the tension that's in the atmosphere the same as I do. You touched on a part of the problem in your speech. That same group of decision-makers that orchestrates the separation, I guess I should say, integration of our schools, they're using the same divide and conquer tactics on the businesses of our blue light district."

"Wait a minute Lucky. I'm able to understand how politics can split up our schools, but the people on the streets; they too slick for a sucker play like that. All of the hustlers know that our only strength is in our numbers as a group doing business together, that's always been our guaranteed bread and butter. People in the mix don't do politics anyway. Why are you thinking that some things are gonna change?"

"Don't be naive, J. Everything that's any thing is handled in politics, that's the problem. As we speak, those downtown hustler politicians and other organized criminal groups have developed an equalizer to gain control over our communities. They've come up with something that will make our people turn against their own mama's. If it works half as good as they expect it to, a brother's life won't be worth a red cent. This new bunch of crooks, they're about to release a new stupid drug called, crack."

In my ignorance, I chuckled and said, "Crack! Ha, ha! Now who in his or her right mind, would want to get high on something with a name that sounds like the split part of somebody's butt? Give me a break."

Surprisingly, and in an unusual aggravated state, she admonished, "Jason, don't play about things that you don't know anything about. You'll be leaving in three days, but in three weeks, that junk is gonna flood our community."

Apologetically, I said, "I didn't mean no disrespect, Lucky. But, it ain't nothing worse than smack. That stuff has made some of our folk' do some crazy things, but our people ain't going totally ape over it. Like I said, ain't nothing worse than that smack."

To my disbelief, with sad eyes, dishearteningly she replied, "It is now."

Silently and attentively, I listened as she told of what she expected to be the cause of a moral decay in many black people and their communities. Informatively, I was told of how international pushers had found other evil people that had created a cocaine-based substance that would be affordable to anybody. The substance would be an extremely addictive commodity, designed with the flavor of the cocaine to be savored; emphasis being directed at the taste buds that can control an already problem riddled individual's mind. The fake candy would be selling as low as five dollars, and soon to be readily available. Lucky, and others in the mix, who held their cultural heritage dear, feared the new illegal substance would create a fixation in black people, one that would ultimately cause them to develop a pattern of erratic behaviors in their life. They'd be willing to do anything to maintain their habit, even if it means for their life to become as an unattended nightmare. When she finished talking, I replied, "You know your business Lucky. If you say this new stuff is that mean, I believe you. But I don't understand. The organization has been keeping smack out of the hood. Why can't they keep crack out too?

"Entirely too much money at an arms reach Jason. I'm only telling you about this stuff so that you won't be surprised when you get back. I want to make sure that you don't get a surprise attack, like a blast from that junk. You and a few other young men that have made good decisions in life are our people's only hope for a future. You're part of that special group Jason. That special group of men that will be too slick to be conned, and to proud to be bought."

"Thank you Lucky, I appreciate that. But in a way that I really can't explain, you've made me sense that I have to have some type of a responsibility, for me to do well. You kind of make me feel like I need to do as much as I can to prepare myself. You almost make it seem like a state of emergency."

Sadly, she affirmed, "You've got the message. But don't you ever forget, you're an original from the streets of our neighborhood, and the underground mix will always watch your back. You're one of us."

With a sense of security, I said, "It's good to know that someone is watching out for you."

"Yes it is," she said. "Many of the members in the mix are like a part of your family, but tonight, I prefer being your friend, just celebrating with you on your graduation day. Plus, I don't think it would be proper for a family member to give you a kiss, not like this."

"Wow!" During that kiss, I wasn't sure whether I was having some kind of a heart attack or what. Inside of me, my body shuddered like an earthquake in its anticipation of eruption, over the soft touch from Lucky's lips. As she released me from her luscious kiss, I gently whispered, "Was that my graduation present, or my going off to, Al-a-ba-ma, salutation?"

Ever so gently, she replied, "Neither, merely another part of your education."

"Well I must admit that it was the sexiest kiss that I've ever had. Is there any thing else you think I might need to learn?"

"I'm glad you asked because, actually, there is something that I want you to know very well. You've got a lot of promising things ahead of you, and since I'm watching out for you, I'd like to make sure that your progress isn't detoured because of some little hot piece of tail. I'm especially talking about the two-timing tramps that might decide to play romance games with your mind and heart. If those tramps want to play, I want to help make sure that you are the best player. If you're really ready to graduate, I'll teach you how to recognize what's the real deal when it comes to distinguishing true love, from what's fake. Tonight, if you're ready, I want to teach you how to keep the ladies happy. And Jason, I sincerely trust that you won't abuse my secrets after you've mastered them, will you?"

The smile that Lucky brought to my face could've easily been mistaken for the moon's glow, as we sped away into the shadows of the night. Lucky and I, along with a condom safely tucked away in my wallet, raced to her uptown condominium suite. My homeboys didn't see me at "The Hole in the Wall" for our graduation celebration. I spent the night with Lucky, and she created a sexual foundation for me to build on for the rest of my life.

CHAPTER EIGHT

I was Alabama bound, riding on a Greyhound Express Bus, to the only school that had offered me a full scholarship. I had no intentions of allowing my aggressive approach towards learning to be dulled by idle time. In an effort to get off to a good start in my upcoming quest, I enrolled for special introduction summer classes. I wanted to take advantage of every opportunity that might give me an extra edge. But before I left home, Bert, Lucky, Jake and many of my other friends assured me they would keep an eye on Mama. After talking with Lucky, I could clearly see that our neighborhood had gotten more dangerous. Mama was single and Evelyn was gone, the extra eyes of protection were like an insurance policy. Although, Mama was not a sitting duck. She'd taught me too much for me to think that she couldn't protect her self. Yet sometimes there is no such thing as being, over protected.

The state of Alabama was beautiful. All along that southeast bound road, I marveled at the mountainous trees and camouflaging colored foliage. Listening to the humming sounds from the motor of the bus, and the tire to pavement vibrations, I found a peace and fell asleep. An hour or so later, my eyes opened and I was awakened by the sounds from the squeaking brakes on the bus as it slowed to a halt in front of an old run down grocery, gas and beer station. The driver announced in a deeply rooted southern accented voice, "We gonna be a stopping here for a while so y'all can stretch and get something to eat. We be a leaving in 'bout thirty minutes, but don't you good folks forget to get y'all some souvenirs."

I stepped from the bus and into a hick country store in a hillbilly town that sold greasy hamburgers. As I ate my sandwich and drank my lemonade, I checked out the place to see how it was set up. The gas pumps had lines to be served and people were buying zoo-zoo cookies, wham-wham-knack snacks, soft drinks, beer and all sorts of other items. Small town or not, that establishment was doing good business. Then I noticed that I was the only person of color in the place, and on the bus too. I didn't become alarmed, but I did become alert and felt a lot more comfortable after returning to the bus. Although as the bus slowly made its departure, I wasn't comfortable any longer. As a matter of fact, I was pissed. From my window's view, my thoughts were elevated into a full-blown rage. Silently, I sat in my seat and screamed to myself. "What's up with this? What in the world is that?"

Up until then, I'd never seen a fully dressed Ku Klux Klansman before. But as bold as ever, there they were. They were lurking around the roadside rest stop, stopping cars and handing out some kind of pamphlets promoting white power. The experience of being exposed to those known haters had caught me by surprise and triggered my first response, one of an angry emotion. Angrily, I reached for the window to shout out any obscenity that might've come to my streetwise mind, but the windows were sealed. I wanted to go kick some butt; however, I had to remember that I was probably the only one on the bus that was offended. Yet surely, if nothing else, as the bus would pass by the hate group, I sure was gonna release my frustrations and flip them the sign, the fickle finger of faith, the soul finger. With anger covering my face as we neared, I made ready to flip them the bird, but Mama's wisdom came to me. She'd frequently said to me, "Boy, Jesus is your Father and don't you let evil emotions steer you toward any other direction, especially through your anger. Don't make it easy for mess to attack you, keep control of your temper. Emotions can lift you to many of beautiful wonders, and they can also drive you into the pits of hell. Feelings of all types will surface, but always remember who is really in control."

As the bus passed, I couldn't help but to stare at that group of stupid people. Those hooded haters were adorned in garments as if they were Satan's clowns. They were nothing like our lovable famed clowns of laughter, clowns like Bozo or Clara Bell. These were evil clowns of doom and gloom, all wet with sweat from the ninety-five degree temperatures. And without a doubt, the souls under those clothes were no joke. It seemed that even from the inside of the bus, I could smell the insane hate that brewed inside of those ignorant people. I sat quietly, boiling over inside, not because of the nut-buckets that I'd encountered, but because I'd let the mere appearance of stupid people in costumes upset me. After all, I'd seen fools before. But my anger was seeded deeper than I was willing to admit, deeper than I could've imagined.

Rolling down the highway, crossing a bridge over the Tennessee River, I looked down to its still and muddy water. Slowly, my eyes lifted to view the river's sandy banks of speckled rocks, and on upward to see her green grasses that rolled through the density of mighty trees. That River sprouted trees that reached up to the blue skies, bringing a beauty that brought me serenity in its infinity. Once I reached a state of calmness, I decided to vent my frustrations by writing a letter to, The Stupids.

Dear Mr. and Mrs. Stupid, and your children too;

Congratulations, you are members of a group of people who can take credit for being filled with more hate than any other group of people that has ever lived on this planet. From my studies in American history alone, you have been clearly defined as a killer of eagles, forestlands, and the buffalo, whales, Native Americans and many other forms of life. Your history shows you as a danger, a threat to every form of life that will not adapt to your enslaving demands. If this was your mission, Stupid, the latest news is that you've achieved it. You've truly become a monster. But I've also got some more news for you, Stupid. Your visions of the extinction of the black race of people are fruitless. I know because I'm one of them, a young, wild, and free stallion that doesn't give free rides to nobody. My back will not bend from your weight, so you might as well just put a muzzle on your out of control antics. You and your confused people may impede some, but you'll stop none.

I'd like for you all to remember this old saying; Love conquers all, as you consider the plight of people of color that live under your rule. Inferior as you claim them to be, they possess the treasured gift of love that you missed. Love has flourished among them in order to override your hate. You need to understand that for my people to have survived through all of the opposition that you haters have put up against us, a strong love for all forms of life had to be deeply embedded in the hearts of our majority. That's the only reason a violent revolution doesn't exist today. As a matter of fact, the only time that I've ever heard the word hate being related to a white person by a black person was when one of them was trying to walk on one of our backs. And that's not hate, just people ticked off at an uneven situation being exercised against them. But remember that Black people do not fear you and we refuse to join in on your hate trip, even if you are a monster.

I will assume that we all know that there's no excuse for hate. Overall, the ethnic group that produced you has proven to be a very productive and beneficial group, and has greatly contributed to the betterment of mankind. They have been able to help the world's progress, in spite of you, and your segregated Klan. Yet, one really can't help but wonder how much more advanced we'd all be if hate were not so vast a trait amid your kind. I ask that you please try to understand that it's not God like when you opt to hate. So, let's praise the Lord, you ignorant bunch of lost followers, and then listen carefully to me. I've got even greater news for you than before. Only this time, it's a message from a child of God. "All haters, your success in shoveling hate has come to an end."

Sincerely not yours;
Jason Philips-Black Man

There had been a gross ignorance on my part in my knowledge of geography. My home city borders Mississippi, but Alabama borders it's East Side. I should've been able to put two and two together and been more aware of the odds being in favor of me being confronted by some racist dummies. By the time I'd finished my letter, the clear ocean blue sky had meshed into a jet-black hue from the darkness of night. I settled back into my seat and thought about why my guidance counselor had tried so hard to persuade me to come to this southern lair. Mrs. Harden had almost dared me to come. She said, "You've got a special gift Jason, but you're going to need to know how to handle yourself and succeed under adverse conditions. You're too comfortable and familiar with how to get over in your, outside activities, like the mess you've been learning in the blue light district."

At the time she was talking to me, I really wasn't ready for a lecture so I started to get up and leave her office as she was speaking. But before I could stand, she admonished, "Don't move boy. Somebody has to be trained to handle the destruction of our people's resources. Soon we won't have stores, movies, clean and safe streets, shops or nothing. As a people, we're headed for the most dependent stage of our times since slavery."

With a sigh, I said, "Please, don't over do it Mrs. Harden. A bunch of us are gonna make it in this world. Plenty of us are gonna own things, and I know for fact that I'm a businessman. I just need to figure out what kind of business I want to own."

"Don't be childish, Jason. Between this Vietnam War, jail cells, and that stinking busing issue, it won't be as many of us left, as you think, not many that truly understand our culture. Many will give in to a lot of the cunning ways of strategy that will be used against us, simply because they can be bought. I don't have documented proof on any of this, but this trend is really right in front of our faces. We will be trained to be something other than what you and I know that we are in truth."

"I don't understand what you're saying Mrs. Harden, what's so wrong with making money?"

From the tone of her voice, it was obvious how much she disapproved of my emphasis on making money. "Nothing is wrong with making money, if you don't have to sell your soul and the rights of other people to get it. Listen to me good. Your Mama has already allowed you to feel the freelance spirit of independence and you've taken advantage of it. You've complimented it with an education and now it all seems to come so easy to you. You still know how to listen to your heart, and that's all I want you to do. Listen to it, then go to Alabama and learn your lesson."

For a while I thought about the point she was trying to make, and then said, "I think that it might be time for a change. You've kind of dared me to do it anyway. Plus, Mama trusts you, and I do too. We both think that you care about me. Anyway, I don't have anything to worry about. You know what the old musicians always say about this town, don't you Mrs. Harden?"

Smiling, she said, "No, I don't Jason. What do they say?"

Confidently, I said, "If you can make it in Memphis, you can make it anywhere."

She clapped her hands together, and said, "That's the attitude young man." Then she added, "Although I must also inform you about something else, just so that you'll be aware. Chelsea University is a great institution, but this is the year that they are forced to meet a quota. The government has ordered them to have a certain amount of black students enrolled. You might be under a microscope. Can you handle that?"

"You mean that they just want me there because I'm black?"

"Yes, that's the only reason. But think about this, Jason. If you did not meet their requirements, you wouldn't have even been in consideration."

"Ump. Mrs. Harden, I'm not sure why you feel this way about me and I'm not sure why I feel what you've said is true, but I do. I make a lot of my decisions based on the solid thinking techniques that have been taught to me by some of this school's good teachers. Mama has also taught me that decisions should come from the heart. My thinking techniques, and my heart, have led me to the conclusion that I should take this test. I promise you that I'll give it my best shot. I just hope that they're ready for me. They've got a piece of paper with my name on it, and I'm going to get it."

Looking outside the window of the bus, darkness from the night reflected as a mirror, showing me on the inside of that Greyhound. I examined my reflection and exercised one of Mama's teachings. I was in control because I had made a good decision. And, I liked the person that I was looking at from the bus window's reflection. After the evaluation of myself from the bus window, I tightly wadded the letter addressed to, The Stupid family, and disposed of it in the litterbag of that fast rolling dog.

Chapter Nine

The bus was arriving at my destination, and in his corn-spun brand of hospitality, the driver announced, "Welcome to Shepherdsfield, Alabama. Folks, thank y'all for riding this bus with us. And the next time y'all take a notion to go somewhere, please come on back and ride this Old Grey Dog."

I hadn't been exposed to the state of Alabama very long, yet I was in awe over her wondrous, natural beauty. Mrs. Harden had given me some impressive information on the school, along with some beautiful photos of the facilities. I expected my surroundings to be totally engulfed with Mother Nature's glory. I really had no clue about the dump of a town I'd just arrived in. That dried up and dusty man-made town called Shepherdsfield, sucked. It didn't fit the scheme of the beautiful tapestry of the land at all. It only spanned for about three dusty city blocks, but I wanted out as soon as possible. The university was about twenty-five miles from the bus station and my agenda was to familiarize myself with its surroundings and acquire dorm accommodations. My timing was on schedule, but I was still uncomfortable in that hick town. I needed a taxi.

Across from the bus station, parked in the front of another one of those all-purpose stores, I saw a cab and headed in its direction. The driver was sitting inside of the vehicle smoking a corncob pipe and listening to some very bad country, Blue Ridge mountain type music. His arm was hanging out of the window, swaying back and forth while snapping his fingers to the beat of the music. I went over and said, "Excuse me. I need a taxi to take me to Chelsea University, please."

Turning his head in my direction and the radio's volume down, the driver said, "You need a ride, I got a cab, and you said please. You is kind of flashy, must be from the city. Anyway, you sound like you might be a good one. I guess I can take you. Let's go."

I was very uneasy with the driver's response. Was he an arrogant man acting ignorant, or an ignorant man acting arrogant? Plus, I wasn't flashy; brothers just know how to coordinate. I didn't respond to cabby's jargon because I really didn't know what to say. But the smell of his smoke made me want a cigar. I thought it might just settle my nerves. So I threw my bags into the rear seat and said, "I need to get some smokes, can you wait for me to go inside a minute?"

He clicked the meter to charge wait time and said, "Sure, I'll be glad to wait. You is new here, better mind your manners in there now, ya' hear?"

That time his remarks put me on alert. I hadn't gotten over my Klan sighting yet; a sense of survival was building inside of me. It had sounded like I'd just been issued a warning by that cabby. Although I did hear him, I didn't acknowledge him, and proceeded to go get what I'd wanted to purchase. Once inside, I saw the store clerk flipping burger patties on a grill and said, "Excuse me please."

The clerk turned, looked at me and smiled. She was just as raunchy looking as the rest of that establishment. Her old burlap material sack moo-moo dress clung to her skin with perspiration from the heat of the hamburgers cooking on the grill, as she said, "What'cha need, Sonny?

"I'd like to have a box of Royal Blunts and a six pack of Canadian Jack, please."

She got my items and returned. "Need something else, Sonny?"

"No, thank you. That'll be all."

She finished ringing up my items, and said, "Okay Sonny, got you all fixed up. But, I need to see some ID. first."

I had graduated high school and was mature enough to enter a university, but not of legal age to buy alcohol. The legal age for buying alcoholic beverages was twenty-one, but if there is a will, there is a way. I'd learned how to make, and had acquired fake identification every since age sixteen. Actually, I didn't really think the hillbillies in that town could read, or calculated well enough to even know the difference. At first, I acted surprised that I was even asked for I.D., and then I readily flashed my adjusted driver's license. The chubby clerk inspected my I.D., looked at me and smiled with her smoked, yellow stained, teeth, and said, "You from Memphis? I like that town."

Not being very interested with her small talk, I said, "I'm glad."

She bagged my stuff, returned my ID and change, winked at me and said, "Come on back when you can now, ya' hear?"

Kindly, I said, "Thank you, and I hope you have a nice day." But as I turned to leave, quick and in a hurry, I bumped into somebody that really was too close to me to begin with. "Excuse me."

The man responded sarcastically and was snickering through a sly looking grin. He said, "You from Memphis, boy? Well, well, well, I sho-nuff like Memphis, too. You know I just love me some of them blues. You people got some good music. It ain't no coon music to me, I like that stuff."

Compliments are fine, but I could smell the beer on that short, stumpy, lumberjack dressed man. He was picking, looking for trouble, and I wasn't in any mood for that. I said, "Buy you some B. B. Bluesman's albums, one of these six packs, and have a good day. Excuse me, please."

He didn't get out of my way, instead, he said, "Now you just better hold on there, boy. You don't know who you be a talking to. Don't no darkies talk to Mr. Jasper like that."

Innocently and in error, I said, "Excuse me, Mr. Basper."

Instantly, his jaws puffed up like balloons and his face turned as red as a beet, as he, also in error, screamed through his snuff filled jaws. "Bastard! Who you calling a bastard, boy?"

That old country boy drew back his fist for a hay-maker-punch that could've knocked me back to Tennessee. But I ducked, and flipped that six pack of Canadian Jack up to replace the space that my face had last occupied. Instead of hitting me, that country dude brought his hand down on my shield of beer so hard that he popped three of the cans tops. As the good old country boy drew his hand back in pain, I put a foot to his vitals. Then, suddenly it seemed that I'd become public enemy number one. Patrons began to pick up bottles and pieces of table flatware. When I saw them coming in my direction, they didn't remind me of the welcome wagon. So, instantly I ran to the rear of the store where the bar was located and jumped over it. I was about to start launching liquor bottles and glasses at that angry crowd like a machine gun spitting out bullets. But to my surprise, when I jumped the counter, I quickly noticed that Alabama barkeepers were just like many others. They too kept a double-barreled sawed off shotgun underneath the bar. I didn't come up from that bar slinging bottles and glasses, but I did come up. "Break yourself!"

I cocked both barrels of that mini cannon and the crowd came to a complete halt, as I commanded, "Make room for me to get out of this dump! Or I'll make my own space!"

That angry bunch dispersed and parted me a way, as I slowly backed toward the door, watching to shoot out the first blinking eye. I had them standing still as statues and completely under control, as I backed through the door and up against the barrel of a Highway Patrolman's thirty-eight revolver. "Drop it boy! You're under arrest."

The officer was not aggressive and I willingly cooperated with him. He wasn't rude or nice. I found that policeman and the department to simply be, indifferent and very professional. Within thirty minutes, I was systematically transported, processed and tucked away into a holding area, charged with attempted murder on the whole crowd in that old run down dump. Then, they put me in a cell, a stinking dungeon for forty-eight hours.

During my stay at the jail, for the first twenty-four hours I had nothing to say to anyone, only to be deeply consumed in my thoughts, wearing the expression on my face that clearly said, "Do not disturb." I had a dilemma on my hands that required much thought. I didn't know exactly what kind of mess I'd gotten myself into, and I didn't think that I'd like to see any mirrors. Yet, looking around me seemed to reflect my most recent decisions with exclamation points. Blunder! Boner! Mistake! I was sure that I'd defeated my own purpose. Although when I finally weighed the pros and cons and reevaluated my alternatives, I came to the conclusion that I'd really done exactly what I had to do. It was most certain that I was not going to just stand there and get beat down by that jerk in the store. That image was a nightmare in itself to think about. All things considered, I had to accept whatever the price. I didn't like what surrounded me, but I did still like me.

Later that day, a cellmate's deep graveled voice rattled throughout the cage, "Ya' wanna smoke?" He figured out that I needed a friend, and for the next twenty-four hours my new friend, Banjo Jones, talked with me until the jailer announced my name to come front and center. It was in the time in between that Banjo enlightened me with his own brand of experienced knowledge. He shared some of his special experienced wisdom with me, accompanied by some of his sweet and soul stirring harmonica music. "Young man, you done gone and put a foot in the sacks of a white boy. It ain't no telling what's gonna happen to you. The folks at this jail, they nice, but you might end up on the work farm. Now, I been a praying something powerful that something like that won't happen, but we both gotta have faith that the Lord heard me."

Banjo kneeled and prayed in silence. He spoke only between God and himself, but he was praying for me. When he finished his prayer, he rose to his feet, reached into his back pocket and pulled out his harmonica. He blew some of the most touching blues that I'd ever heard. The expressions made from his music allowed me to feel sadness turn to joy. Then brother Banjo took the instrument from his mouth and said, "That was because you from Memphis and I know you already homesick. It was also the prayer that I prayed for you. I wanted you to hear my prayer speaking through the sound of music. That way, you can know what it means to you from the way it made you feel."

"Thanks Banjo, thanks for uplifting my spirits. Just met you, but I gotta call you a friend."

"Now that makes an old man feel mighty good. It ain't too many young people listen to nothing any more. You just remember that it ain't nothing that music and prayer won't cure. Even if you don't know how to do neither one good, both of them still gives you a little extra special fuel for the soul to keep on pushing. A little bit a go, I heard you praying, so I know you know Jesus. But I want you to feel the joy He can bring you when you talk to Him through music. It kind of helps when thangs so tuff that you don't know what to say. Little brother, I want you to have this music."

Intensely, he gazed upward as I sat, captivated by his words. Stretching his hand to me, he offered me his harmonica, and said, "I want you to have this, boy."

His shared wisdom and talents had honored me, but as he reached out his hand and presented me with his harmonica, I didn't feel deserving, and began to say, "Ahea, come on man. I can't ta——-."

Swift and unexpectedly, Banjo put a finger to his lips to interrupt me, as he spoke. "Hush, little man, don't go spoiling my pleasure in giving with your city ways of thinking. You're getting this 'cause, one way or the other, you got a battle ahead of you and gonna be a needing all of the help that you can get."

I accepted his gift and marveled at the intricate works of the well-crafted instrument. "Thanks Banjo. I can't play, but this will be a treasured keepsake."

"Keepsake, learn to play it boy. Just blow in it and see how easy it is to make music. Ain't no such thing as a bad note, unless you play too many."

I smiled at the old gentleman, and said, "Banjo, I was born and raised in the home of the blues, but you're the most intelligent blues man I've ever heard."

"Blues man! Son, I ain't no blues man. I'm God's man, an old-fashioned country preacher."

Stunned, I said, "I'm sorry, I didn't mean no harm, got much respect for you. I just meant to say that you play a soul stirring music, and you seem to be full of wisdom. That's all I was trying to say."

"I see what you mean, but let me tell you 'bout old Banjo. My music is my praise, part of my life. Listen, if you can put the pieces together that I'm 'bout to tell you, you're gonna know a lot of truth. The name Banjo, come from my Daddy, it be his name. He was the best cotton picker in the fields. He picked cotton so fast that they started saying his hands moved faster than a banjo picking man. Banjo, that's just my way of carrying on Daddy's name. A man gets power when he honors his Father. When you can understand that, then you be ready to carry your own cross. I can tell that you a good young man, just done run into a detour. That ain't no dead-end, God is just trying to teach you something. He'll let you finish your mission, but me, well now that's another story. You see this here old country preaching harmonica man done killed one of them hate filled folks. One of them got too far out of line. That's my cross to carry and Jesus is the only one that can forgive me. But look at that old harmonica, you know it's too pretty to be locked up."

Banjo's folk wisdom and spiritual spun food for thought would be used throughout my lifetime. He was also able to offer from his perspective what was to be expected of black people by white folks in the surrounding county. He said, "This County only tolerates the shuffle butt black people."

My friend made me realize that under the conditions he'd described, my streetwise and arrogant attitude would be thoroughly tested. When time came for me to depart my cell, I played three notes on my harmonica, turned to Banjo and said, "That was the prayer that I will be praying for you. You know what it means from the way that the sounds made you feel. Goodbye, my friend. God bless you."

The jailer led me up front, returned my property and released me to one of the university's representatives. The ignorant man that had provoked me earlier had also been carrying a gun. It was found under his lumberjack shirt at the hospital while he was getting stitches for his hand. The arresting officer testified to the judge and I was released, ruled self-defense. I was pleased and relieved to see a university representative waiting at the jail to offer me assistance upon my release. He said, "Hello, my name is Mr. Craig. I'm from Chelsea, here to help you get settled. We're very sorry about the problems you've experienced. The board of trustees has reviewed this matter and understands what happened. Come along with me and I'll help you to get situated."

That gentleman was pleasantly accommodating and I welcomed his assistance. He took me to the administration building, guided me where I could receive my dorm assignment and waited for me. He also took me to my room, made sure that I was okay and all prepared for classes. But, he never once, shook my hand. I wasn't sentenced to jail; I'd voluntarily sentenced myself to an unsociable institution. I was confused and didn't know how to deal with the unpleasant feelings of rejection. I'd been emotionally scarred by the existence of prejudice being directed at me. Although, as time went on, I was able to clearly see why Mrs. Harden had been so adamant about me being very cognizant of Chelsea's bachelor's degree program. The school was an innovative university that had incorporated a group of business professionals who had developed and administered a careful synthesis of combined traditional and career education. The school offered courses in the inner workings of different corporations business proposals and strategies. The staff at the university all seemed to have the same objective in preparing students for the work place, corporate ready and managerial competent. I was well taught and tried to absorb every iota of knowledge.

I was also able to see why Mrs. Harden had warned me to be on alert when dealing with Chelsea's social climate. Indiscreetly, I was tactfully and constantly reminded that I was not a welcomed addition. I was treated as if I was only a numbered statistic toward meeting a quota for the university's annual equal educational opportunity government reports. I felt like I'd been forced upon the school, only pending the threat of a newly enacted federal legislation called Affirmative Action. Most of the student body, faculty, staff and administrators gave me the impression that they desired to see my head stuffed into a part of my body where the sun never shines. Even my ten fellow enrolled black brothers would shy away from me, but they'd jump at every opportunity to suck up to people of other races for their acceptance and favor. I was very lonely at that place and became introverted, humbling myself to the isolation. With me being surrounded by disguised hatred, I drew strength from the bits and pieces of scripture that my limited church attendance would allow my mind to recall. I wasn't as well versed as my hometown Reverend Clark, I just called on Jesus and told Him that I loved Him, and I knew that He loved me. Suddenly my lonely feelings diminished as I sat in silence. Yet, considering the real reasons for my undeserved segregation, my attitude towards my abusers was simple. There is no man that doesn't like me who deserves to be deceived by me into thinking that I liked them. I became obliged not to associate with those that possessed a prejudiced hatred against me, just because I was a Black man. The lackadaisical attitude at the university toward racial injustice should've been criminal. But, since I'd come there to earn a bachelor's degree in business concepts, like it or not, my sentence to that institution was for a minimum of one hundred and fifty eight semester hours before I could complete the school's undergraduate program of Business and Industrial Engineering

Technology. The under-the-breath mumbled insults from overbearing, ego-tripping and trying to be intimidating professors, plus the local red necks in the surrounding county would all have to find a way to deal with me. I was there to graduate.

People who have never experienced true freedom are happy to receive any. But, those who have experienced it will accept nothing less. In the past, my world from within the confines of an established community of Black people had shielded me from the direct punches of racism. That neighborhood allowed me to know the scent of freedom and I wasn't about to accept anything less. To combat my dilemma at Chelsea, I used the wisdom given to me by my respected neighborhood elder, Mr. Charles S. Flag. I'd promised him that if ever I could make a difference, I would. So if I was considered to be the man of the future, it was time for me to make ready.

The first thing I wanted to do was to learn more about becoming a good man, a good Black man that was not going to be played on like a chump. I started preparing myself by closely scrutinizing American History so that I could see how people had been manipulated over the years. I was able to learn the rules of some of the games that tricksters had played on us. Games like unequal housing rights, insurance redlining, FBI covered-up scams, drug infiltration and many other devious plots. If history was to reveal the way out of an unfavorable past, Chelsea would bring me up to date on how to be a champion at playing the new games of the current times. I wanted to calculate my moves against those social cheaters based on their own system. For my entire stay at that university, I used the same approach to learning as I'd used at E. K. Waymon High. Like an ostrich, I buried my head in the sands of the knowledge that was being offered by the institution's professors and dedicated myself for success.

My major learning focal points were the wheeling and dealings of the various phases of corporate insider communications. My area of interest was in mastering conglomerate strategies and their methods of training to control and monopolize. I wanted to understand how they could successfully get rich, and still remain evil without being exposed. In order to gain full understanding of the nature of that greedy beast, filled with prejudice against black people, I stayed in that hostile environment of Shepherdsfield, Alabama without one visit home. My decision was made easier when Mama decided to move in with Evelyn and her family. They needed Mama and she needed to be close to them because Evelyn was pregnant again. Chelsea became my own personal training ground, as if I was in basic training for the military. I found ways to tolerate my situation and successfully accomplished my mission. Finally, I earned enough credits to receive my degree. I didn't want to participate in their graduation ceremony because I had no respect for the school's disregard for human rights. So, I opted to wait for my BS certificate to be mailed to my house. As soon as my requirements for graduation were met, immediately, I bought a ticket on the next express dog to Memphis.

Chapter Ten

There is no space that is more comfortable or accommodating as home. It's the place where success originates, and if there is disruption at home, whatever else that transpires in their life will ultimately have a major void. When all seems to turn sour, home sweet home has to be available for a retreat, a place to regain one's sanity. I'd witnessed marvelous sights of nature's beauty that graced Alabama's terrain, but I preferred the faster pace of being at home in the city. And although I was at home alone, home was still a welcomed sight.

Morning came and it felt great to awaken in my own bed. "Ring, ring, ring. Hello."

"Hello, Son. I called the school and they told me that you had left. Is everything all right?"

"Hey Ma, everything's just fine. I left school a little early, but I did graduate."

I could sense her feelings of joy, as she said, "Well that's great, I'm so proud of you. Although, I do think you should've stayed for the ceremony."

"Mama, I really had stomached about as much of that school as I could stand. They're going to mail me my degree."

"I believe you did best. After all, you're the one that had to put up with their mess. The main thing is that you finished."

"Thanks Ma. It helps me to know that you understand how I feel. Tell me, how are you and Evelyn's bunch doing? Tell me about the new baby?"

Mama was thrilled as she proudly proclaimed, "Yes indeed, we've got another baby girl and her name is Clara. Now that Estelle is over her cold, I'll get you some pictures of your nieces. I've been teasing Evelyn, telling her that Clara has a head shaped just like brothers."

Both of us had a good laugh over that, and then I said, "I can hardly wait to tease Evelyn about that myself. Baby Clara has got equipment to be a good thinker."

"Just like you Jason, a good thinker."

"You sound happy to be a two-time Grandmother. But I guess I can boast too, I'm two times an uncle."

She laughed, and said, "I'm very happy about my granddaughters and I thank Jesus for them both. But I'm not ready for you to make the grand baby numbers increase."

I quickly assured her that my additions would come much later, and then said, "I'm glad that you called Mama, but this is long distance, tell me about the rest of the family before we run the bill up too high."

"Ha, ha," she laugh and said. "I see you've still got your Father's dull sense of humor. But all is well here Son. Estelle is over her virus, Evelyn is out shopping, and Daniel should return from an officer's briefing in the morning. I'm doing much better also, now that I know you're all right."

"Now Ma, you know I'm gonna take care of myself. I'm not going to let you down."

Instilling her confidence in me, she said, "You never let me down, and I don't believe that you ever will. But, I do want you to leave those ugly thoughts back at Chelsea. Don't think that I can't hear the sounds of weariness in your voice. Remember that it's over and you got what you went there for. Don't carry the weight of what it took to get your degree any further. Drop it and move on. There are still many things that you have to do in life, like finding a good job so you can make all of that hard work pay off for you."

Not to let her know the emotional stress that I hadn't gotten over, I said, "Mama, I want you to stay and enjoy yourself as long as you like. I love you, but I think Evelyn might need you more, helping with the babies and all. And now that I'm home I can keep the house in good shape, and the crab grass cut. I'll be just fine, now that I know all of you are okay.

We talked for over an hour. It was like she had understood that I needed a comforter. After our conversation I had a cup of coffee and began to analyze the uncomfortable things that I'd noticed during my taxi ride home from the bus station. If I hadn't known any better, I would've wanted to be pinched into reality and awakened from a bad dream. But, I wasn't dreaming. The city, my town, reminded me of a larger version of Shepherdsfield, Alabama. It looked like a dump. The area around our house was still nice, peaceful and seemed safe, but the majority of the other areas that I saw were very neglected. Stores were all boarded up or had bars as decor, and trash was just blowing with the wind, up and down the roads. I was very disturbed, yet not ready to investigate and see to what extent the deterioration of the community had manifested; I only wanted to enjoy the comforts of my surroundings at that time. So, for the next five days I stayed to myself, not as a shield to protect me from the evil; I just wasn't ready to face what I'd sensed in the air about my people. Lucky's predictions had become a visual reality.

Saturday came and the groceries ran out, time had come for me to crank up my old car and make a move. Yet, the further I drove; more needles seemed to pierce my heart. There were no more of my favorite soul food restaurants. The structures were still there but they were dilapidated. People of another culture owned them now, but they still called the style of cooking, Down Home Country Southern. I even had to by my groceries from a store with ownership that could barely speak my language. Places that I'd purchased fine clothing from in the past, they now sold dry goods with loud and gaudy colors that looked to be made of cheap material. Where our people once were banking, now stood a pawnshop. And worst of the lot, too many of the homeboys that I saw while driving, were junkies. Quick and in a hurry, I returned home, but not before salt was poured into my wounds. I passed by my old Alma Mater and it was closed. Now, it was a boarded up eye sore that was being used as a refuge for drug dealers, wine drinkers and other derelicts of society. It made me wanna scream and holler, to see what had been done in such a short span of time to my peoples life style. I didn't want to see any more.

When I returned home, the sick feeling that I had inside of my stomach was relieved when I saw my high school debate award, proudly displayed on our fireplace mantel. It was a beautiful replica of my school, etched in gold, with ruby, onyx, and emerald used for the representation of the school's colors. My nausea softened as the plaque seemed to restore my sense of pride. That award and my thoughts of recent accomplishments achieved at Chelsea, reinforced my feelings of being a top achiever. But being a top achiever was merely another of society's terms that confused me, just another term that I had to define from within myself.

A top achiever is considered a winner in this society and there is usually an award when the apex is reached. Olympians win gold medals and boxers wear championship belts. Actors get Oscars and many other world class achievers receive a variety of other awards. I felt a part of that elite group because I'd gotten my awards, a diploma, trophy from high school, and my degree from college. I am an achiever. But now, just like many other achievers who've reached their goals, a reality sets in and you're left to wonder. Where do I go from here? At that stage of my life, I didn't know which direction I should take. I could've easily entered into the corporate world. To enter that career arena, the process was simple, "When in Rome, do as the Romans." I'd follow the procedure, just submit resumes, set up some interviews and select my best offer. That was the American way.

Even though I never grew to like Chelsea University while I was there, I did grow in knowledge and would've been an asset to any company. I'd been well educated in that institution of higher learning and had gained excellent people manipulating skills. But at this juncture, I had to make a decision between using my skills to address my own materialistic wants and needs, which corporate America could easily provide, or to address the problems of our community. Yet looming in the back of my mind were the people that I would have to associate with to climb America's corporate ladder. What if I was to become a conglomerate, CEO? If I were to be hired as an executive, surely I'd hate to be forced into a social environment with so many people so unlike me. I was well aware that successful corporate executives are totally consumed with their organizations. It's almost like they have to marry the company to become successful, and I most definitely would hate that. But what if nobody contacts me at all? Will that dictate if I eat or not? What if I am contacted, like the offer, but not the foul climate that emits from their biased environment? Will I bend over for the money, or stand proud and erect, poor and all alone? Yet to guide my thoughts, memories from my past advocated a different philosophy. What if hell freezes over? Who cares? I'm not going there, or to anybody's job either. I loved my people and grew angry from the thought of me losing sight of the importance of our sense of township. Then too, what if I do opt for devising a plan of restoration, and fail, leaving me with nothing? Although when everything is all said and done, for me, chances were always dilemmas of uncertainties that I never feared.

I remember an old saying that goes; "You don't miss your water until the well runs dry." Well, my brothers and sisters in Memphis seemed to have become arid. The south side of town was the well that had quenched the thirst of our community for the safety and prosperity of our people. Now, the well of the south side was bone dry of anything considered to be good. It was in need of a stick of dynamite to prime it for a renewed flow of water. While I'd been away in Alabama, I'd felt the despair of being a stranger in a strange land. My experience at Chelsea University had taught me that, as a person of color, I really wasn't welcomed anywhere, except at home. Unfortunately, my once strong community, the source of my growth, was dying. Even though I really didn't know if I'd been destined to change things or not, I did know that somebody had to do something. Also, my heart couldn't sit still and wait for others to come save us. So, out of necessity, my task became a mission of restoration. Even if I didn't succeed, I'd at least plant a seed for the progress to develop a plan for the needs of a crippled group of people. Also, I figured that my people have worked and grossed major capital for almost every ethnic group in this country and now it was time for the profits to come home. I'd been away for a long time and only a few days had gone by since my return. I hadn't even visited any of my old friends yet. But with all things considered, I opted to do a quick assessment of some of the major problems that I'd recognized in the city. I found the difference between the Memphis I'd grown up in, and the one I was experiencing at that point in time, as different as night and day. The physical appearance of the city seemed as if it had sprung up ghettos faster than ragweed could've grown. It had become a town never to be called city beautiful again, not anymore. Worst of all, it was surely a town with too many of my black brothers and sisters walking with the limp of a lost since of pride and having no unity among them at all.

I concluded that there were two major issues I knew would have to be addressed before any progress could begin. The city officials had incorporated a system that had locked the doors of opportunity for black people in the city. I'd have to find a key to open that door, or kick it down. The other major issue attributed to our regressive state was that stupid drug called, crack. It was the source of the demise of our self-esteem. But, the major obstacle to be faced in order for us to relieve our selves from that, monster drug, wouldn't be the junkie; it would be the hustlers that sold the junk. Surely, I'd have to find them other moneymaking opportunities. Yet, in spite of the obstacles, I became determined to blow up the well of my community and let the arid people from our city's south side quench their thirst with the taste of nectar that was once removed.

As I analyzed my situation under the circumstances, my arrogant nature began to become insulted by the memories of the past and present atrocities that have been committed against my people. It irritated me to no end that in her entire history, America hadn't ever let any race of people remain destitute and suffer from a lack of opportunity. I wondered, why had she chosen to abandon mine? Yet in reality, I knew that America was being governed by politicians, but managed by major conglomerate executives who are controlled by well-known gangsters. So, if gangsters were to be an indicator of who would be running our country, it was clear to me why Black folks hadn't gotten a square deal. America was being run by a bunch of cheaters.

If the phrase, up a creek without a paddle, holds any truth, my brothers, sisters and elders of today were floating out of control. Our communities of the past had once lived by an old adage of wisdom proclaiming; it takes a village to raise a child, but now they'd been turned into a divided wasteland, a ghetto for us to raise up our young people. If God were willing, I was going to restore that united village concept. As bad as things in the neighborhoods had gotten, restoration had to become a matter of survival for our people. I was determined not to allow the newly discovered atrocity to manifest. Yet, unfortunately, I had to assume that Charley Flag's theory about assistance from my people, the well to do and elite among us, as not being available. I figured that if they were going to do anything positive, it should've already been done. From the conditions that I'd witnessed, they were not going to do anything, unless they knew that it was going to make them some more money.

I was well aware of the fact that I needed money, but I needed loyalty more. To acquire them both, I played my trump hold card, the one that Black America had kept palmed. My recruits and resources would come from the underground mix. It was the place where only the strong survived and the quick thinkers excelled. Those veterans, the old heads in the mix would be my trump card. They were always looking for a brother that could turn big money into more, and still be trustworthy. With them, my reputation would precede me because I'd already established trust among them. From within the ranks of the mix, I'd be able to get all of the help and money that I would need to get started. I was certain that the members of the original mix of people would welcome a chance to get their illegal situations restructured into legitimate enterprises. Through a blending of their resources of hustlers, con artists, and other big money players, I could bring about a cohesive merger between the best of my street education, with the best of my university education to make society's rejects become my assets. With that theory as my trump, I'd be able to cut a path through the dense forest that I saw ahead of me.

Chapter Eleven

Keeping true to the nature of my mission was going to be a key ingredient for the success of my idea. I had to be honest and nothing could be selfish about my motives. My intentions needed to warrant the building of a legitimate situation, with illegal building blocks. It was necessary for me to find a way to repel the expected temptations that would come my way. At Chelsea, I'd allowed my exposure to racism to form a, not-so-nice, attitude towards our society's majority. Easily, such a non-productive viewpoint could distort the thoughts generated in my vision's ideal. My acquired knowledge from the university, combined with the resources of the underworld, would offer me weapons enough to make my vision a reality. But also, the guidance to stay on the straight and narrow was vital for me to have. Mama wasn't there with me, but her wisdom was. Inside my mind, her wisdom guided me to Peace in Faith Church. I went to see Reverend Clark, because for me, a sincere spiritual discernment was in order.

"I'm pleased to see you, Jason. Welcome home."

The Reverend and I enjoyed talking about the good old days, times when he and other good neighbors played active roles in the up bringing of kids from within our community. Because of his positive interventions in my life, he and I had developed a healthy respect for each other. He knew me very well, well enough to say, "Son, this church hasn't seen your face since the Sunday before you went off to school. I can still remember you coming to the altar for prayer, asking our Lord to protect and guide you while you were to be away. But, if I recall correctly, it had almost been a year since I'd seen you in our pews before then. Although it is a joy to see you now, I do not believe that this is just a social visit. You didn't come here to just chew the fat. What kind of help do you need from Peace in Faith? What has caused you to grace our doors?"

"Well, Sir. Some things are going on in our town that I just don't understand. You and I both remember the way things were, and we can clearly see the community's digression. All of the pleasant memories of my childhood, the independence, secure surroundings; caring supervision and nurtured teachings seem to be fading away. All around me, I feel the spirit of progress for our people being dampened. Reverend, I want to revitalize that progressive spirit. But before I can make an effort to correct any of the problems I've seen, I need your view on what has happened to our life style of being a thriving village community."

"Unfortunately," he said, "I can't tell you exactly what has happened to put our people in this position. Over the past few years there have been more confusion than I can comprehend, and certainly too much evil."

I could see the pain in his eyes as he did his best to reveal to me the mystery behind our dilemma. Carefully, he explained that fast money, deviated morals, drugs and a devastating lack of self-control, were the roots of the problem. Although much of his assessment concurred with what I'd already assumed, he revealed yet another reason for our reversed progress. Sadly, he said, "Things began to become unstable shortly after you went off to college. When the responsible citizens noticed the infiltration of bad elements, we asked our Commissioner Gains to run for mayor. He was our knight in shining armor, a qualified candidate with our best interest at heart. Because he was so well liked and supported in our community, he was a shoe-in candidate for this district. Committed to not allowing our communities to be over run by crime, he ran on a solid platform addressing violence and the trafficking of that demoralizing drug they call crack. Our man was a true thorn in the side of his opponent. Then, all of a sudden the opposition dealt us a hand of cards from the bottom of the deck. They went on the north side of town and found a respected and familiar Oreo Brother to run against our man of the hour. That sly and slick scam tested the unity of our people of color. I'm sorry to say it, but that was a test we failed. Consequently, our vote was split and a once distant white horse won the election. Surely, that was a bitter pill to swallow. What really threw salt into our wounds was that three days after the election, our Commissioner Gains was gunned down. Now, left with no qualified leaders to guide our people, an onslaught of evil engulfed our villages, giving those murdering cheaters their desired results. When all of the dust finally settled, we'd divided ourselves and were made an easy prey for the wolves. I only pray for a remedy before it's to late for recovery. Yet considering your sudden visit to Peace in Faith, and your obvious concern about our situation, do you think that you may be our remedy? Do you have a way of addressing this dilemma of destruction?"

Not really wanting to reveal that I even remotely had a plan, mainly to avoid it from being scrutinized during it's infancy, I emotionally said, "'I really don't know. Right now, I don't have any answers. But, I do know that I ain't gonna roll over and take it on the chin like a chump. This backward trend cannot continue to develop without someone attempting to stop it. I don't know exactly what I will do, but I will do something."

"I'm pleased with your passion for righteousness Jason. Although as I hear the anger in your voice, I must remind you that this church cannot condone violence."

"I do understand Sir, and please allow me to assure you that even though things may erupt, I'll only entertain the thought of violence to repel the violence that confronts me. During the years that I was away, I learned that fighting fire with fire is a poor strategy. A more effective strategy would be to throw water on it, and let it exhaust itself. Actually, the reason for my visit with you is to ask for prayer that will allow me to develop discretionary nonviolent tactics. If I'm going to attack the evil that we both know is at hand, spiritual discernment will have to be my compass."

With the caring demeanor of a proud and trusting father, he replied, "It's good to know that your priorities haven't changed. I'd truly hate to believe that all of the time I spent teaching you had been in vain. Although, I must also say that I don't know why you've chosen this as your mission, but I'm happy to see you address our problem. This town is in need of leadership that can fight, pray and not be bought. We need a leader with love in his heart, instead of hate. To truly be real about this matter Jason, you could've very well been God-sent for this situation. After all, the description that I just gave of a good leader depicted what I think is your true character."

"Thank you Sir."

"You're welcome," he said. "But don't thank me so fast. The commissioner had those qualities also, and he was defeated. You don't have a plan, and as we know, you're up against a skillful demon. Odds are that you'll be swallowed whole."

In a slightly rebellious tone, I said, "Then maybe I'll have to rely on my faith for direction. Just keep the faith, that's what you always say makes things work."

The Reverend smiled and said, "Boy, you've still got a hustler's reputation around here, and if I didn't know you better, when you talk about faith I'd have to laugh. But there is more than one side to you. There is a difference in what you show the world, and what I know is inside of you. I know how hard you've tried to always do the right thing. Over the course of your life, I've seen you walk that fine line between good and evil, and you've always seemed to ultimately make the right choices. God has watched over you Son."

"I believe He has. Please let me reassure you that in spite of the unique experiences that I may have had, Jesus will still determine my priorities. I promise you that as I strive to reach my goals, I'll never pay the cost with the price of any lost souls."

"Your assurance is comforting, in these days of deceitfulness, the church needs to feel trust in the people that we choose to help. You just remember that I'll minister to a leader of men, only if God leads the leader. Now that we're both on the same page and have an understanding, let me plant a seed of knowledge for your victory. Maybe I can help keep you from being blind sided, like we were with our plans for Commissioner Gains."

Surprisingly to me, Reverend Clark began to point out what he felt should be my weapon of choice. He said, "I want you to focus on those unique experiences that you just referenced. I've known you all of your life, and in many ways, life has given you opportunities to acquire different sorts of wisdom. When you were younger, you were my most avid Sunday school student. Then later, as you grew up, you got hooked up with that underworld group and became a star pupil with them. Between that Fast Eddy and that woman, Lucky, you learned from the best in this city. I'm still amazed that your morals didn't get demonically corrupt, and I'm gonna give your loving Mama credit for that. Also, before you left us, you showed us another side of yourself by becoming an honor student. Now, with a degree under your belt, you're returning home with a compilation of knowledge that's equivalent to the most learned of the prestigious. Son, this combined knowledge of your unique street life experiences, and your formal institutional education, blended with your spiritual awareness, has equipped you with a force that's more effective than violence could ever be. You've developed the power of persuasion. You're a manipulator of people, a person that can change the mindset of others. These are traits that politicians dream about having, and dictator's fear coming up against. This is an effective weapon, but it can work for you or against you, to be used for good or bad. It's truly a weapon that can cut both ways, just like a "Double Edged Sword". Always remember Jason, a man can live by the sword, and does not have to die by it, only when he allows our Lord to wield the weapon. If this is the weapon that you'll choose for fighting our Goliath, Peace in Faith will diligently pray for your direction."

Peaked with a newfound inspiration, I said, "Thank you for your words of wisdom, this is the kind of guidance that I came for, and will continue to need."

Assuring, he said, "I'll watch out for you and do my best to make sure that one edge of your sword is wielded through the wisdom of Jesus, and the other through your knowledge of his presence. And for you and those that you will lead, take this scripture to heart. I pray for your victory, Psalms 149:6, "Let the high praises of God be in their mouth, and a two-edge sword in their hand."

From the depths of my soul, as I left the church, I realized that a man could do God's work even if he doesn't regularly attend church. Although, the man has to allow church to regularly attend his heart.

Chapter Twelve

The place that I used to contact my main recruit was also one of my favorite places to party, and fortunately, it was still in operation. It was called, The Living Room. A very prominent place in our city, It was an upscale after-hours R&B spot for the elite of our society and the underground moneymakers among many people of color. The establishment was a prime place to make business contacts, a made to order starting point to recruit for my new project. It was also the best place in town to enjoy talented rhythm and blues musicians. "The Living Room" offered me a friendly and familiar place, where I could find my old friends from the track, at least those that were still alive and well. The old heads in the mix knew me from way back when, and the new crew on the scene knew of my reputation as being one of them.

At The Living Room, when I first walked into the club I knew one thing for sure, the person that once said, business and pleasure don't mix, had to be on a different page than me. There was no doubt that I was there for business, but with that blues band kicking, and the crowd throwing down on the dance floor, I was also going to have a good time. Over the past few years, my quest for knowledge had been satisfying and rewarding, also an uphill struggle. The pressure from it all had reached a peak. But while listening to the music in the ambiance of the evening, I settled into a comfort zone and began enjoying myself.

The timing for searching for my prospects was perfect. That night at the club, a special VIP celebration was being hosted. It was a showcase conference for the regal, non-taxable, and non-corporate moneymakers, a convention for those who make a living in the underworld. That annual event was a rare opportunity for competitors and adversaries to flaunt their success. The gala was a chance for them to show off their diamond rings, chrome-trimmed cars with golden-rimmed wheels, glittering gowns, fancy shoes, and tailor-made suits. I also was definitely dressed for success, and to impress. I wasn't new to that scene and knew how to handle my appearance. Although I may not have had very much money, I made sure no one could tell it, not just by looking at me. I was always dapper, suave, and sharp as a tack.

The festive mood of the gala was overwhelming, but time soon came for me to change gears and take care of some business. I didn't have any time for half stepping, so I set my radar to seek out the top dog, the one person in the underworld that could influence the rest of the pack. Actually, I knew him very well, about as well as he knows me. I can still remember when he pitched pennies on the street. Now, he launders money, hundreds of thousands at a time. And for me to pave the way for the success of my dream, I need him. The mark for my arrow was my old running buddy, Bert Crane.

The crowd was thick, but I finally managed to maneuver my way to the kingpin's table. As I caught his attention, amid his entourage of beautiful women and king-sized bodyguards, I greeted, "Word up, Brother Crane. What a brother got to do to rap with an old homeboy these days, buy a ticket, or what?"

Along with a smooth low-five slap, he replied, "Good to see you. My main man J.P., its been a long time. How about grabbing a seat and joining us?"

I took a seat and he introduced me to the rest of the table. Politely, I responded to them, then again turned my focus back to Bert. "I see the dice have finally started to roll you a few sevens. Looks like you really got it going your way. You're in the big time. You're living large, brother."

With a smile of satisfaction, he said, "You know how it is my brother. Life has been tough, but it's been just as sweet, but I hear you're the man of the hour. The underworld knows 'bout you getting your paper from the place. Congratulations, you represented us well. The wire even has it that you gonna be the next CEO to come from the street."

Waving off that idea, I said, "Correction, Brother Crane, here is the latest news flash. The wire should read the first CEO of the streets."

Bert's smile faded as he looked at me and said, "Slow down brother, don't go throwing me no curves like that. You got the big ticket, a paper from one of the man's best schools. Why you talking 'bout taking back to the streets?"

It wasn't hard for me to relate to Bert's reaction. To him, and many others in his world, a person making it from the streets and into a legitimate mainstream moneymaking situation was like beating the odds. In some ways, I was a small ray of hope that represented them. Their world of prosperity was often short-lived. In street moneymaking, longevity was never really expected, and all knew that to be a matter of fact. So, I tried to set his mind at ease, "Ease up my man. I ain't talking about reverting back to the jungle; we both know the ending to that story. But, you know me, I'm always thinking and I've always got a plan. Bert, I've got a plan now; I'm here on square business. I came specifically to see you."

"Well, what it is dude?" He said, "What do you need me for? I'm in the mix, and if you don't want to be in that, what did you come to see me about?"

Considering the noise level and other distractions in the place, I decided to hold off on trying to explain my plans, and said, "Listen up, brother. I don't want to throw no chill on a party set like this. To tell you what time it is with my plan will take a little privacy. My game tonight is only to make contact. It ain't a secret that out here, you be the man. I want to let you know that I've got an idea for a brand new mix. You know that I don't play. I'm still singing that same old song from yesterday, rapping straight up and down business. I need you to call me tomorrow at home. We'll find some time, and I can run it all down to you then, you know what I'm saying."

At first he looked at me with a blank expression, then he said, "Sounds like you been doing some heavyweight thinking brother J. And, if I remember right, you always been the man with the master plan. Maybe it just might be worth my time to see what this new thang is all about. But if nothing else, you and me can at least catch up on what each other's been doing the last few years. Gimme your digits and be at home, noon tomorrow, I'll talk at you then."

I reached into my coat pocket and flipped out a business card that read, Jason Philips-Businessman Extraordinary. I handed it to him and said, "Very good, partner. I'll just consider this a wrapped up package."

We sealed our appointment with a low-five slap between the two of us, an agreement that must be honored, even between thieves. Yet unknowing to him, Bert was about to become a major player in the success of my plan. My business at The Living Room was done and I was pleased that everything had gone as well as it did. I was also happy to be headed back home, because the alcohol I'd drank was about to start making me feel stupid. Finally, I reached the walls of safety at home, took a deep breath, exhaled and drifted into a sound sleep.

Chapter Thirteen

Morning came and soon, the phone rang, "Ring, ring, ring. Hello."

"What's up J.P.?"

"Everything is everything, my man."

Teasing, he replied, "Now, tell a brother something good enough to have him awake this early in the day? I hope you got a monster of a plan for me to be out before dark."

I laughed, and said, "You old night owl; I bet it has been a while since you last saw your shadow. But homeboy, open your ears and check this out. I've got some performance graphs and other track record data on some great companies that can be acquired. This is confirmed information with promising speculations on how much money can be made. But for you to be able to understand the theory behind this venture, we need to meet. Bert Crane, I've got a plan, trust me. When can we meet?

I sensed it in the sound of his voice that he understood something was about to happen, he just wasn't sure what. He said, "Last night you said that you didn't want to be in the mix, but now you talking like you already in it. Are you sure you ain't getting ready to play ball in the man's backyard? You confuse me, J."

"Its time for a new game Bert. It's time to do something legal."

"Umm." He said, "It all still sounds mixed up to me, but it don't really matter anyway. I'm sure you know better than to contact me without a plan to make money. Let's hook-up, dude."

That's what I needed to hear. I said, "When we meet you'll find out that something special is about to be in the wind. Tell me what's up with the hook-up? When can I see you?"

"Well I ain't changed; I'm ever ready, twenty four hours for seven days a week. As a matter of fact, I'm only fifteen minutes from your place right now. When you hear a horn toot, come to the door and I'll be there."

"Hold the jive, and the con-rap, don't play with me. We both know that you only blow your horn at chicks, tricks and chumps. I think you better come to the door, and knock like people who getting ready to do business are supposed to do."

"Just a test J., I knew I couldn't run a play on you. I just wanted to see if you still had some fire left in you, or if that school had taught you to sell wolf-tickets. But I'm still gonna toot, 'cause I got something real special for you to check out. And wipe that stone face off your mug before you come to the door."

"OK man, I don't mean to sound so uptight. I guess I'm just a little excited about my plan. This is some serious stuff I'm fixing to try. But anyway, I'll be listening for your toot."

Fifteen minutes later, I heard the toot from Bert's horn. It sounded more like three-part harmony coming from a band of trumpeters, rather than a car horn. When I opened the front door, I could only stand in awe. In front of my house was a stretch limousine, a chauffeur at the wheel, and Bert leaning against its fender with an ear-to-ear smile plastered across his face. That luxury vehicle was a true testament to his accomplishments. Complimentary, I said, "I like your style, Mr. Smooth Operator. But, now that I've seen your new toy, come on up and give a brother some Dap."

Bert raced from the car to the porch and we exchanged our special Dap greeting, a greeting just for brothers. Dap, was the name of our fellow homeboy handshake. It was a sincere, and aggressive form of a ritualistic type of embracing; using sequenced rhythmic hand movements that were synchronized to end with a tight handgrip and a hug. Those Dap handshakes were part of a rite toward unity among those closest to us as friends. It was a very special way of greeting each other that had been brought back, and shared with us by our brothers who had suffered in those battles fought in the Vietnam War. The greeting was a kind of exchange that showed love and respect for each other. After Bert and me finished showing our respect, he stepped back and said, "Man, you don't know how good it is to have you back. I kind of missed you."

"Its good to be home. I'm glad I was able to run you down. It was a sure bet that you'd be at the party last night."

"You got that right. It ain't nothing worth talking about in this town bigger than that convention. And ugh, I guess you noticed who was, Top Dog?"

"Sure I did. Its like I said, I went there to contact you, Top Dog. I've got a plan."

"Well you came to the right man. Come on and lets hear about your so called, real deal."

My buddy and I hadn't spent time with each other for a long while, and I was sure that we both had plenty of experiences we would like to have shared. But at that time, we both knew and understood that it was time to deal. We went in and sat at the kitchen table, where I dished up my prime question. "What happened to our town Bert?"

"J., you know that I deal with those hood-rats every day. Man, they be living like share croppers, and still buying that dope, rotgut alcohol, and some woman's favor. Every day that goes by, they ain't doing nothing but living to have a good time. In a way, I guess I might be just like them. I ain't been doing nothing but looking out for number one. I can see the dirt, but I over look it, cause I've got plenty juice, and been getting paid some mad cash. Last year, I made money like I owned IBM or something. And today, I run all of the businesses in the blue light district. Plus, when everybody in the hood, that we used to think were respectable, suddenly began to move, I figured that was the rule of thumb for the days and time. Something like, every man for himself and God for us all. That's really all I know about what's happened. But tell me what's your mix all about J.? What's on your mind that can make some of my games change into legit enterprises?"

In my mind, Bert's comments registered him to be filled with pure greed, but in my heart, I knew he preferred things to be the way they were, before the demise of our community. I spoke to him from my heart, and said, "I'm not trying to make a new proposal that'll make you any richer. You probably already have more money than you know what to do with. My new situation is designed to form a conglomerate."

Perplexed, he stared into space and said, "A what?"

"Be patient, man, I went to school with you, I'm gonna explain. A conglomerate is a mass configuration of a variety of businesses, with confusing identities of ownership. I want to form one for us, as an entity that will allow for longevity of capital. And in the process, with our newly generated profits, I want to put the pieces of our community back together."

"Well," he said. "You gonna have to break that one down more than that. I don't know what you just said man."

Sharply, I reminded him, "You might not ever understand what the word conglomerate means, but don't act like you don't remember how this city was when we were growing up. The dollar bill might blind your eyes, but I know that the vision in your heart is twenty-twenty. So, don't act like this junkie's paradise is something that you like living in."

"Look J., just because I'm making good money don't mean that I can be changing things. That's like cutting off my nose despite my face. I make my money off those suckers out there. I can't help it because they stupid."

Bert had done very well for himself, in his assigned roles, with many of his underworld enterprises. But I wanted him to see that his little world could come tumbling down at the drop of a hat. I needed him to see that, although he was doing well, he was still working for someone else. Also, I'd have bet a dollar against a donut that he wasn't working for a Black man. Yet, it was clear to me that a gambler, such as he, was not concerned about the risk of being involved in any well-planned business venture. Bluntly I said, "Stop complaining and groaning. I was trying to tell you last night that this is a living large plan, ain't nothing short term about it. It's the chance for you to break legit. Sure, you're making some long money, and you gonna keep making money, because suckers are born everyday. But like I said; you ain't gonna own nothing. Man, can't you see, ain't nobody taking care of the neighborhood anymore. Getting some more of that whack crack dope, that's about the only thing you can get two brothers to agree on anymore. You probably sell them most of that crap."

"Hold that thought, J.! We ain't kids no more, and you can't slick talk me into doing thangs like you used to. In today's time, I'm Top Dog, I run stuff now. Anyway, you just got home, why you think you know so much about how to fix everything? You don't even really know what time it is."

I calmed my emotions, and then said, "I don't mean to sound pushy, brother, I'm just tired of not being welcomed as a person, anywhere in America. I can remember a time when this town had a lot of people that worked very hard to make this place a welcomed and safe haven for us. Now it's a dump. You'd better recognize what has happened since the cheaters have taken over Alvin's Burger Hut, Ed's Beer Barn, Jack's Rib Rack, and every other place that ever made money for our people. Today, black folk can't figure any way to make money, except for selling them foul drugs. You can act like you don't remember, since you getting paid. But you, Bert Crane, you owe a lot to the folks that watched over you, especially Reverend Clark. He kept you out of jail more times than you even know."

"Whew, you're right man. I might not know how many times that preacher stood up for me, but surely, it was more times than I can count. Although, I do remember that every time he talked to Dad, my butt would need a pillow."

"Well," I said. "I think your butt needs something right now, if you can't see the need for us to get back to the basics. Our village community has to be reestablished, along with our life style of being a responsible people. Do you understand me, or am I gonna have to tell Reverend Clark to have a talk with your Daddy again? Bert, If we don't have a place to call home, a place where we can raise our families, and develop our culture, we ain't gonna be no better than a bunch of new day sharecroppers. If we don't do something, we'll always be working for somebody else, and never owning nothing."

"So what are you saying we should do? Are you and me supposed to rebuild the hood, or what? That don't sound like no joke to me, and it don't sound like no plan. That sounds like you been dreaming."

"If I'm dreaming, please pinch me so I can wakeup. Man, I wish that I were dreaming. Maybe then, when I open my eyes this nightmare of a neighborhood would've disappeared. But, that ain't gonna happen because I ain't dreaming. And this ghetto, it ain't gonna disappear. Man, somebody has to do something."

Sarcastically, yet promising, he said, "Well it sounds to me like you already got thangs figured out. Man, you talkin bout building a little city, and running it. I can see tomorrow's headlines saying; "Extra, extra, read all about it. Jason Phillips and his Chocolate City are rising to power and gaining international recognition." But wait a minute J.; let me ask you this. Are you sure you ain't gonna have to have an election to pull this stunt off?"

"You're a funny man Bert. Can I take that day old joke as a yes to you helping me?"

Seriously, he said, "I'm gonna help you because you my homeboy, but let's get real. Both of us know that if we try making those kind of changes, we gonna piss off a bunch of people."

"Plenty of people just might get pissed off," I said. "But we won't be one of them, they ain't that slick. The hood was taken from us; we can take it back. That, ain't no joke."

"Man," he said. "I been knowing you a long time and I don't think nobody else know about some of your smooth moves but me. On the real side, J. you're an honest and smart brother. I believe that if anyone can put the pieces together, of this screwed up puzzle, you'd be the one. You got my vote, partner. And if your deal is really real, about helping black folks, I can get good money. It's plenty of people in the mix that will be happy to back you. Actually, them that can make a real difference, they already know you anyway. But, this deal of yours is a sho-nuff heavyweight deal. The people downtown, the politicians and thangs, they've always let some brothers make some money, but they ain't never gonna like it when we want to get some ownership. This deal of yours is deep, a world changing deal, and for a deal this big, I've got an advisor. If you're ready, and all of your ducks are in a row, I'll make a two-hour turn-a-round trip and come back with my agent. Then, we can see if you really want this pot of water to reach a boil, or if you were just blowing off some steam."

Confidently, I assured, "You're a day late and a dollar short. I'm boiling and ready to cook, right now. But what can you tell me about your agent?"

"We do deals together because we got trust; everything else is a secret from me. All I know is my job. I collect money, follow orders and keep the peace in the district. I trust you J., but you've been gone a long time, it's some new games being played today. This meeting with my agent is gonna show me if you can still work in the dark. I need to see how well you can handle yourself these days, see if you can still improvise. Plus, if I'm gonna risk my fortune, I wanna be for sure that you still sharp enough to handle the unexpected."

Truth be known, in many ways Bert had been right about one thing, I didn't have a plan, I only had a dream. I had daydreamed that I was going to manipulate others to create what I felt was right for black people. I may not have had a plan, but I could clearly see my dream well enough to make up a proposal. I was sharp enough to fake it. I said, "Take your two hours, just bring me back somebody that can read, add, and speaks English better than you do. I'll have something ready to show your ace agent."

Bert and I laughed as we ended our conversation, then he headed west in his stretch limo to usher his counterpart to my calling. I didn't have a clue as to what kind of a person he'd be returning with, and wasn't sure of how I could fully express my concepts of the need for unity among Black people, with someone that I had never met. But, I was well prepared to illustrate my dreams of financial success, even to a stranger. I was confident that I could show that a major profit could be gained from my ideas, because teaching the art of creating, operating and maintaining successful corporate entities was what Chelsea University had become nationally acclaimed for. While there, I'd been taught very well.

One of the school's practices for students was for them to study the practices of existing successful corporations. Students were allowed to select the companies that were to be studied. We were asked to simulate a companies management operation, and develop strategies that could improve the profit ratio. I'd selected companies from within the surrounding areas of my little world in Memphis, and had amassed in-depth files on the profit and loss trends of profitable business ventures. My files consisted of surveys, case studies, statistical data, and a myriad of other materials on their profit and loss performance. And, I was secure in knowing that all of my information was progressively sound. Those nutty professors at school had closely scrutinized all of it. They would've given a right arm, died and gone to hell, just to have proven my innovative business theories to have not been sound. Yet, in spite of those that stood to derail my progress, I maintained my, 4.0 grade point average, and graduated from that renowned university Magna cum Laude. Ironically, I was now planning a take over, and going to use my newly learned skills to lay the foundation for creating a better place for Black people to build their futures upon. With my well-scrutinized data, I felt that I was more then prepared to meet Bert's, or anybody's agent. I was well prepared; all I really needed to do was find something to wear that would insure me of making a good first impression. So, I selected my well-tailored gray silk blended corporate office styled suit, along with a simple black crew neck pull over shirt. And, when I looked into my mirror, I was pleased. But, also as I was looking into the mirror, an alarming thought crossed my mind. My entire concept was being spearheaded because I thought that Black people needed a booster shot to uplift them. In my mind, I knew that my purpose was for the betterment of mankind. Yet in reality, I also knew that people have narrow perceptions about many things. I had to realize that a great number of people might call my project, "A Black Thang." The thing that took me off balance was the fact that maybe, just maybe, Bert's ace agent might be, a white man.

Chapter Fourteen

"Ring, ring, and ring. Hello."

"Get ready J., its game time."

Twenty minutes after the phone rang, Bert's limousine came to a halt in front of my house, and I stepped out on the porch to greet him. The driver opened the car door, and Bert got out, soon to be followed by his agent. Surprisingly, his agent generated an aura from within me that I was unable to closely examine, yet given no choice but to acknowledge that it did exist. Trying very hard not to stare, I stood in somewhat of a daze as I viewed a Cleopatra look-a-like step from that stretch automobile. She was a very distinctive and successful looking woman. Her hair was pulled back into one of those cute little, ball kind-of-a hairstyles, enhancing her facial cheekbones and casting a soft silhouette, as though it was a crown being worn in the sunlight. She was a well-dressed lady, professionally attired in a navy blue, knee length executive styled business suit, tastily accessorized with navy blue stocking covered legs. And to accent her whole persona, she wore a pair of blue suede shoes, with medium heels, that made her stride flow as smooth as a ride in a Cadillac. I witnessed beauty, as I thought, "Umm. Bert's ace agent is certainly not, a white man."

"Jason Philips, meet Miss Regina Mallory."

For a brief moment, my mind had taken a trip to wonderland, featuring Miss Mallory with her deep skin tone of midnight black. In my short dream, she was yearning my company, but the urgency of business stabilized the intoxicating attraction that I was feeling. Sobriety came and I extended a hand as I said, "Pleased to meet you." Then I invited them inside and we briefly exchanged some pleasantries before settling in the den to address my proposal. I gave Miss Mallory some of my pre-selected files for her scrutiny and was sure that dollar signs would be an impressive way to start our relationship. As she reviewed my schematics of profit loss calculations, I summed her up.

It wasn't unusual to find women with control over some of the business aspects of the mix. Some of them even controlled large territories, and being attractive didn't give them any brownie points or extra credits. Everybody in the mix had to earn his or her positions by being qualified. But to me, this Miss Mallory didn't seem to be old enough to have gained such status; she was younger than I was. And how in the world did beauty ever become representative over the beast. Bert, he was simply a mystery to me. It seemed she should've been working for him. At some point and time, these were questions I'd need answered, but for now, I sat at my desk and tactfully began to introduce my proposal. "Miss Mallory, I've asked for Bert's assistance in helping me create a legitimate financial networking system, one that will allow the flow of money to funnel through a conglomerate, controlled from our developed schematics. It will be an operation that will allow for longevity on our earned capital. If you're able to find my project to be sound, Bert suggested that you may be able to help me. Also, I'd like to thank you for your interest and your time."

"You're welcome Mr. Philips."

"Please, call me Jason."

"Ok, Jason. I respect Bert's judgment, and if he shows interest in a proposition, I'm willing to give it consideration."

"I can appreciate that. Have you had enough time to scan the projection totals?"

"Yes, I've scanned them. You show an unusual mixture of diverse business combinations. Even if they turnout not to be profitable, they do still seem interesting. But your concept is an old concept, one that has failed, time and time again."

"Ugh," unsettled, I said. "I'm sorry, I don't understand. Can you tell me more of what you're referring too?

"I'll be more than happy to tell you more," she said. "You see, the principles of the combined businesses that you've targeted, show you leaning toward an exclusively black enterprise. That's an old concept that has only worked on paper, sort of like these sheets of paper you've given me. And even though the profit projections look great on the surface, and very well could work; Bert and I already have money. He told me that you had something different. But this, old concept, it all sounds too familiar to me."

"I'm sorry that we haven't met before, Miss Mallory. Fortunately, Bert and I already know each other and he understands my special expertise. I know how to arrange and rearrange the pieces of a puzzle to make them fit. I'm what every business needs, a problem solver. The Black people in this city have a problem that I'd like to make an effort to solve."

Sarcastically, she replied. "Getting rich off black people. Now that really is an old concept, Jason."

For that fiery and aggressively outspoken lady, I had to put on my game face, as I said, "Miss Mallory, please allow me to explain something to you, maybe then you can tell me a better way of approaching this proposal. I truly do want you to understand my plan." As she settled down, I continued. "First of all, there are a couple of ways that I have in presenting a proposal, and the method really depends on who I'm presenting it to. I do it one way when I know that someone else has final approval. I do it a little differently, when I'm dealing with the person that's in charge. Tell me, please, whom am I dealing with? Who is who, and which method should I use under these circumstances?"

My questions struck a nerve in her and I could almost see steam rising from her head. She became stern with me and made direct eye contact, as she said, "Let me paint you a picture, Jason. I'm a low profile person. Bert, he is the number one man on the street, and he knows his business. He directs all of the deals that go down, they go through him. He directs all of the major players and blue light businesses. Also, he handles his people well. But the kind of action you're planning takes place in this town only, if and when, the white collar and politically oriented people allow it to take place. That's where everything within the underworld mix really originates. That is also where Bert stops. I play that hand. I'm the dealer in that game, and that's why I'm here. If your deal is going to fly, it will be in my airport. I'm the hold card in the games played today. The ace of spades."

Bert sat looking as if he was awaiting my reply, while I tried to look as if I hadn't just been slapped on the wrist for getting my hand caught in the cookie jar. I said to Miss Mallory, "You've definitely answered my question. Maybe now, we can bring this pot to a boil. Those facts and figures that I gave you represent my position on a few choice small businesses that have some problems. If you look at their profiles you can clearly see that the problems basically stem from mismanagement. They all have potential, and are currently available at bargain basement prices. We can incorporate them to create a network...."

"Excuse me," she interrupted. "This still sounds very familiar. What makes you so different? Exactly what makes you think you can change anything?"

"I've got a quality that's rare to find these days. I'm a businessman in the truest sense of the word, honest and in love with my people."

To my rescue, my buddy finally broke his statuesque pose, and said, "Wait a minute Regina, let me say something that might help you to see his point better. You see brother J. and me, we done did a lot of things over the years, but he's just like me, a man of his word. He can be trusted. If he say something, straight-up-and-down, you can take it to the bank."

When Bert finished, Miss Mallory stood, walked over to me and said, "Out of all the master minded, do-right projects I've been exposed to, honesty has been the missing ingredient, most probable cause, for the down fall of them all. But still, I can calculate your proposal's data and it all translates into cash. Remember, we've already got cash."

I had to call on my patience, then said, "I'd like you to understand that I'm not really trying to show how much money I can make you, only that you're not risking any. I'm trying to show you how we can gain freedom for Black people by creating, a win-win situation. Nobody has to lose. But, I do understand your attitude of disinterest; it's well justified, considering that you haven't heard me out. Please allow me to continue, without you taking it personal. This is general information, even though it's true. You, Bert and many others, might have plenty of cash, but can't none of y'all cash in your black skin. In this phase of life, a time of blatant suppression of our culture's growth, even your money won't buy you a friend, or a neighbor that likes you. Take a good look around. It ain't a majority of any group of people that likes you. And it's only because of your color. There's not one culture that considers your existence to have any real value. No group on this earth needs you, and they would like for you to feel the same. As sad as it may sound, too many of our own Black people, don't like each other, or themselves. We can't live in individual vacuums; somebody has to build a renewed sense of pride, purpose, hope and opportunity back into our people's way of thinking. The concept of my vision is to rebuild our community. Memphis needs a facelift. Bert and me can remember this place once being a haven for black people, a real land of opportunity, and that's what I intend to reestablish. By the grace of God, that's what I will do. Miss Mallory, your skin radiates a beautiful shade of black, and you have a lovely head of wavy black hair. You're a very attractive woman. In my eyes, you're a queen from the Nile, a true beauty born in America of African heritage. But in reality, in this USA and around the globe, you're just black. Even with your cash, you're still black."

I had to still myself; it dawned on me that my emotions were getting in the way of my sincere proposal. To insult Miss Mallory with my choice of words would've been self-defeating. So I took a deep breath, and offered, "Would you care for something to drink, Miss Mallory?"

"Water, with ice, and please, call me Regina."

It was a good thing for Regina to accept my offer, and from her response, I gathered that some of the first impression tension had begun to ease. Bert had listened while slumping in the lounge chair, he requested, "You got a beer?"

"You, you can step for your own brew, you ain't no guest. I ain't been away from home that long."

Now feeling very much at home, he said, "I'm right behind you dude."

That was just what I wanted him to say. I stopped the presentation for us all to get a breather, but with Bert in the kitchen, it made it hard for me to cool out. He kept jiving me about how his agent was basically, eating me for lunch. Once we returned, Regina took a sip of the water, and surprisingly said, "You've really got big plans. I'm going to do a compilation on the companies you've studied and see how they may be incorporated with what already exists. I'll contact you through Bert when I finish my evaluation. Looks like a good and resourceful flow of capital can be generated, but it still looks a lot like you're going to be playing a game; The return of the spade. Actually, I don't think that you really have a clue on what you're gonna do next. But, I think it might prove to be interesting to see what you can do with an opportunity."

I was very impressed with Miss Mallory, even though I was asked to wait for final approval of my proposal. I felt good about our first meeting and Regina had been a welcome relief. It was a pleasure to talk to a woman without an identify crisis. And as for Bert, he had done exactly as I'd expected; he came through for me. After they left, I really didn't want to, but for the lack of a more convenient choice, I went and got me a plate of food from that, so called, down home southern country cooking kitchen joint that was run by people who couldn't fluently pronounce, sweet potato pie. Then I returned home to a movie, and a good night's rest.

Chapter Fifteen

The next morning I was awakened to a bright sunny day by the ringing of the telephone. "Ring, ring, ring." Bert's voice was on the other end.

"Hello."

"J. P., I've got good news this morning."

While still half-asleep, I said, "Well, I can't think of a better way to wake up. What's up Bert?"

"You made a good impression last night. Man, I even like where you're trying to go with your idea. And Regina, man, she just bombarded me with questions about you."

"That is good news, but can't you tell me a little something about her? Gimme an edge, dude, something for me to work with. What's up with that chick?"

"Sorry bro. I told you before, can't tell you much else 'bout her. That lady's business has been shielded from the wire. But talk to her yourself, you the man with the plan. Anyway, I'll tell you what little I know, just don't ask me no more. We've been working together since just 'bout the time you left. She came to town with built in power. All of a sudden, everybody was going through her for everything. She made me her middleman so she could maintain that low profile of hers. All I can tell you 'bout her is that, on the real side, she's been like a pot of gold to me. And on the real side too, if you talking 'bout helping the black people, she straight up and down 'bout that."

I accepted Bert's reluctant, and limited information about his agent, and said, "I guess I'll just have to take your word on your agent's reputation. Now, let's get down and build us a foundation. Can you give me a general run down on how businesses have been handling their security and protection? When we get started, there will be some objections, and I want to be ready to address them."

"Makes perfect sense to me, homeboy, cause if you plan to do as much as I think, some folks gonna more than just object, they gonna put a hit out on you."

"Yeah, you're probably right, man, but that's one of the main reasons I need you. You know what time it is, give me the run down on the strong-arm crew. What's up with the protection?"

"Alright," he said. "I'll give you a break down on security, enforcement and protection. I control all of the business around the blue area, and it ain't no need to go any further with that, but there is another side to the coin. The man you really need to get on board has control of the people. He already has a close knit group of followers and they're looking for ways to clean up the drug trash in the hood."

"Ugh, excuse me, but ain't you part of that trash, Bert?"

"Ugh nothing, that's cold, J. It ain't like that, man, ain't the same thang at all. Regina and Me got our hands deep in the drug market's money barrel, but we make our money from supplying it to folks that wanna have a good time, not them losers who committing a slow suicide. I might be making some money dealing drugs, but even I agree with the folks that say smack, and crack, got to get out of the hood, if you gonna build anything that's good. I agree with you, J., we gonna have to show these hustlers how to make money on something else. The guy I'm telling you to see knows what time it is on that deal too. Like I was saying, he's been trying to come up with some kind of plan to take back places that's been invaded by the dealers. They want to open up some stores and stuff, like it used to be. This guy even got little army squads tucked away in strategic places. In a lot of ways, they kinda be on the same mission we trying to focus on. Plus, this fellow's people trust him, and are very much so loyal to the cause. But in my honest opinion, he ain't sharp enough to be a good leader. Y'all need to see if y'all can hook up and help each other."

"Yeah," I said. "He does sound like someone that I need to meet. Who is he? Can you arrange a meet?"

"Certainly I can. He's easy to find. But, take note on who he is. It's Archie."

"Well," I said. "Who is he?

"J., it's Archie."

"Who? I don't know anybody named Archie. Is he black?"

"He's as black as coal, and you do know him. Archibald Benson."

I shouted, "T-Roll! Archibald Benson, a.k.a. T-Roll! Bert, we don't need a maniac."

Hushing my outburst, he said, "Wait a minute now, J., just calm down and listen up. You need to go see the brother; I'll make the hook-up. He camps at the old Ritz Theater, corner of Hall and McLee Street."

"Bert, are you really sure that we're on the same page?"

"You bet we are, buddy. But, when you go to make the meet, see what's real, not what was in the past. This is a new day, and he is a different person. Hook up with the brother, we can talk about it later. Ok? Also, I forgot to mention it, but the meeting between us, and Regina, its on brother. 1010 Rosewood St. Suite #20, Plaza Building, tomorrow night at eight. Okay buddy?"

"Man, you sure are full of good news this morning. Hook me up with T-Roll and we'll see what's up. And when we meet tomorrow, I need you to bring me layouts of your territory so I can make some updates."

"All right dude, I'll bring them to the meeting. But before I leave, I need to let you know something. Brother Archie, he don't answer to the name T-Roll no more."

"Thanks man, I'll remember that."

The Ritz Theater once was a source of family entertainment. They showed all of the first run movies starring black entertainers, and sold the best corn dogs in town. Now, it was a fort, with fenced in surroundings, bars across the windows, and a gated entrance. I rang a buzzer on the outside of the gate to acquire access and was answered with a shout from behind a closed door. "What do you want?"

"This is Jason Philips. I need to talk to Archie."

The voice didn't respond, but the door opened, and there he stood, Archie, alias, T-Roll. He was all dressed up in a white, oriental, self-defense uniform, fitted with a black belt. Silently and solemnly, he beckoned me through the chain linked fence entrance, and through a dim lit lobby, exposing an impressive training facility. Areas were sectioned off to accommodate both offensive, and defensive hand-to-hand combat tactics. Some of the sectioned cubicles hosted instructions in a variety of weapons expertise, ranging from assault artillery, through an assortment of homemade explosives. The facility also incorporated several classrooms that taught an untold history of the Black experience in America. And, to shield his operation from complaints about noise, Archie had the entire complex sound proofed. Although when we entered his office, I was even more impressed not to see it filled with black power propaganda. Instead, it displayed educated black men of respected principles. Men like Mandala, Garvey, Frederick Douglas, Martin, Malcolm, and many others. We sat at an oval conference table, and he began to say, "Time is out for the war between you and me. Bert gave me the run-down on what's up with you, and I believe that you're for real. I also believe that with the right kind of help, you can take charge of some things in this city. But exactly what do you want from us?"

I could only look him in the eye, and say, "Whatever it takes to get our village community reestablished, that's what I want from you and your group. I'm being as straightforward with you as possible, Archie. If Bert has briefed you, then you already know that I'm going to be taking on a ruthless band of heathens. I need you to follow my lead for progress, no questions asked. I need you to get the job done, with no explanation of how. You asked me what do I want from you and your group, now you know. What's your response?"

He almost stood at attention, as he saluted me with a raised clinched fist of unity, and said, "Word up, my brother. Progress is the main mission of my group, and if it's evident in your plans, it'll speak for itself. So, if you say whatever it takes, you've got it."

I returned his salute, and said, "Thanks brother. The dust will be flying soon for those that have a foot on our progress as a people, they've gotta go. But, do you and I have to remain this formal?"

"It is a new day Jason, and I'm surely a different man. A few years ago when I left this town, I was meaner than a junkyard dog. Then, I got shot up over there in that war, and it wasn't long before I found out what it means to be alone, and scared. That was when I discovered, brother-to-brother love. Basically, we all survived because of each other. I've been peaceful every since. Now, I'm only mean towards those of evil, and I have not forgotten how to be that way. I just want to exercise that nature of myself on the deserving, and not the innocent."

"I'm glad to see you've made a turn-a-round from being the kind of guy I remember. But since I know how you were, I also know that you can handle what I'll need done. I need to be totally honest with you T Roll. Excuse me. Archie, I need to be totally honest with you. I'm feeling my way through this whole thing. Actually, I'm making this plan up as I go, but if we can stick together, we will make this thing work. Are you okay with that?"

"Man," he said. "I already know what you're all about, ain't no need to prove nothing to me. It's long past the time for us to get on with this over due business of making our community self-sufficient. Together, let's build us a new hood to call home, even if we do have to stumble a bit." We exchanged our offering of friendship, the rite of Dap. I left that theater feeling I'd incorporated an army, and that a friendship of old had reached an apex. Between Archie and me, the hatchet was buried.

After talking with Archie, Bert and his agent, I concluded that there were others who were highly concerned about restoring our communities. It was a good feeling for me to know that I was not alone in my quest.

Chapter Sixteen

While I still had some daylight, I continued my recruitment search for more prime soldiers, and the next mark on my target was my happy homeboy, Homer. He had done well for himself, owning and operating a bail bond agency. And if I wasn't sure about any part of my plan, one thing was for sure. I knew that however my project was going to shape up, Homer's business was most certainly going to be frequently needed.

"What's up homey, J! How has life been treating you?"

"J. P., its good to see you man. I heard that you were back in town, but I didn't expect to see you so soon. What's happening brother?"

Homer and I reminisced, joked and laughed. Briefly, we just shot the breeze between two old friends. Then I asked, "How did you know I was back in town?

"You're on the wire, man, I thought you knew. Word is that you're talking about doing new business with the people in the mix."

"Oh, I didn't know I was on the news. Anyway, the word ain't quite right. It's close, but not right. I've got some things, some ideas that I want to get started. That's why I'm here talking with you. I came to see you because you're my homey, and I'm trying to find some people to work with me that I can trust. I need your help, buddy. Will you work with me?"

"Man, as far back as you and I go, you know I'm gonna roll with you partner. And being in this bail bond business, I sho-nuff know how important it is to find somebody that you can trust. What do you need a brother to do, J.?

"I've been asking everyone that I talk to for their take on what happened to our town, and how so quickly. What's your spill? What kinds of patterns have you seen?"

Homer shook his head in dismay as he concurred with what I'd already heard. "Man, it's really the same old games being played over. Some outside jerk organizations with deviated intentions spread money, money, and more of it, into the hands of a select group of Oreo brothers. Those sell-outs, began to sell out their businesses and encourage others to do the same. They all shouted, "America is great. I've got my piece of the pie, now you go and get yours." Then they all started to move to the other side of town, leaving their shops and stores to be owned and operated by profit concerned people who had no vested interest in our people's growth. Those profit-oriented businesses were of diverse groups, but they all banded together to learn how to become experts at one thing. They all learned how to suck the money out of the neighborhoods. Sometimes, it even seems like they think that us Black folk are as disposable as paper cups. They want to drain our brains dry by keeping us high, picking our pockets clean, and then just throw us away, into their garbage can jails, and lonesome graves."

I could tell from the fiery look on Homer's face that his passion for the loss of our community's unity, matched mine. I looked toward him and said, "I'm afraid that was my assumption, but I did like the way you explained it. Actually, what you've said only reinforces the need for my plan, and my plan is to reverse what has happened. But first, I'm gonna try to get together with some of the people in the mix to show them how to convert some of their money into a legit operation. I need to show them how to make some cash without going to jail for it. Although, the real deal, I ain't told nobody about it, not yet."

"Well, I for one am glad you're addressing the issues. I don't know if I really believe that you can do anything about them, but you can count on me to help you in any way that I can."

"Homer, who put me on the wire?"

"Man, it was a chick named Miss Mallory, she put you there. Man, she's the hottest thing that has come through this town in years. She seems to be in charge of everything now days. That's an important lady; she's the reason the word on you is getting around so fast. Her instructions are for everybody to be expecting you. They're also instructed to listen, and then make up their minds on if you're a sham, or not."

It was a positive thing that Miss Mallory had given me an introduction, before actually giving me an OK. But, I also took it as her way of testing me to see how well I could take advantage of an opportunity. Assuming that all lights were green, I said to Homer, "I'm building an organization and the odds are that many of my people will have a few run-ins with the law. I want to be able to assure them that they won't rot in jail. Plenty will go, but I want you to be able to make sure that they don't stay. Can you handle that? Better yet, will you help me?"

"Man, with good money, my staff and connections can beat any charge that ain't got an eyewitness."

"That's just what I need to hear, but there is still one thing I could use as soon as you might be able to get it."

"What it is man?"

"I'd like a full take on your, Miss Mallory. I need you to take it to the limit, nothing routine, you know what I mean."

"Wow, that's a tall order you be asking for buddy. It ain't nothing routine about her. That lady has got so much juice that ain't nobody been able to put all of the pieces together on her. But, I'll do my best. As a matter of fact, I've got an ace in the hole downtown. My buddy, Ike, he's close to the sheriff and I'm sure he can pick up some of the loose ends."

"That's great, but Homer, I need you to dig deep. Do your best, and I'll do the rest. Also, today my business is on the wire, but tomorrow it's going to be more private. We're going to work through a chain of command. Your people will be your command, you deal with them, and then you deal with me. Man, we can't be naïve, spies are still the number one tools used to divide and conquer a good man's plan. I need you to watch my back, brother."

Happy Homer gave me one of his famous clown smiles and said, "Well, now that sure does sound like you're cutting me into your new mix in a major way."

I said, "Partner, I'm telling you, if you stay righteous, and black, we can ride high."

"Alright J., I get your drift, and I'll have the information you need by tomorrow, straight up at noon."

I went home and reviewed what had turned out to be a very productive day. Like a child in a toy store, I was excited with anticipation over what was going to happen next. Morning came, and then noon, and once again, I was at Homer's agency. He was so busy shuffling papers that he didn't notice I was in. I got his attention, "You got my information ready, partner?"

"Hey man, you bet I've got it. This should be plenty, but it ain't all. That Miss Mallory seems to have a Chicago connection that we can't trace. What I have for you ends at the beginning of where that Chi-town organization cuts us off. My man, Ike, says FBI is the only way to go for any more, but I think what we were able to find will help you some."

I took the file from him and gave up a low-five, as I said, "Thanks man, I'm gonna make this do."

Once at home, I almost wore out the telephone. I talked with homeboy, after homeboy, and got leads on other homeboys. Great responses were received from them all about cooperating with me in the development of a village concept. Now, the only thing that was left for me to do before the big meeting was to study the Mallory papers. Considering her earlier remarks, when I'd asked whom I was dealing with, an impressive report on her was anticipated.

Regina Constance Mallory was a well-versed, educated lady that was raised in a single parent environment. Overall, the report showed her to be indirectly connected to the most powerful of our city. She had all of the people in authority at her disposal, and they had given her control of all of the black owned businesses that had over a two hundred thousand dollar profit. Around the town, she was known to most people as heir to her family's wealth of, so-called, old money. But in reality, it was new and established gangster money. This money and all of the deals that were being made with it were filtered through Bert. Our society's influential and prominent, as well as its underground elect, both knew Him as collector and enforcer. Neither world could connect Miss Mallory with any illicit activity. The files showed that she was born in Memphis, but raised in Chicago with her father. He had been a long time force in that city's organized criminal arena, and was currently on the run, suspected for his involvement in the conspiracy to commit murder. Also, through his wife's underground activity in Memphis, police had linked, Jack Mallory, as the hit man in the untimely death of the opponent that ran against the current Mayor of our town. The timing of the death of our political candidate seemingly coincided with the takeover of power by Bert's ace agent.

Things became clearer to me. Miss Mallory knew who had ordered the hit during the Mayor's race, and was using it to control her status with our city's leaders. Her undisclosed information was so secret that, even our underworld had made some type of an agreement for her not to reveal what she knew. And from what I read about her, I believed that she knew a lot, as well as how to handle it. Yet, in many ways, I felt something in common with that lady of power. She and I were both walking close to the edge of the fine line that our society had drawn between legal and illegal activities. I found it very impressive that I was able to draw the conclusion that, in spite of her power, she had refrained from taking advantage of innocent people, and had only cheated the cheaters of our society. I had a gut feeling that she could be trusted, but not mistreated. She was not to be mistreated because, it was obvious that she had the power to make a person, permanently disappear. Yet, at face value, I believed her to be someone that could also make me a qualified and trustworthy partner, but there was still one thing I didn't understand at all. If this lady was born in my town, and worked the streets, I should've known, or someone that I knew should've. Although, as I continued to read more, the mystery unfolded it's self through her mother's profile. The profile of her mother showed her making intermediate visits from Memphis to Chicago, but law enforcement agencies never had any proof of her being involved in any wrong doings. Her name was Constance L. Mallory. But, to our police department, underworld gangster contacts, politicians and business leaders, she was a well-known and high profile street hustler known by her alias, Madame Lucky.

The news about Lucky saddened me. From the implications of the contents of the report about her obvious involvement with the national gangsters, I knew her only options. When you're in hot water with the law, and the mob too, you either fade into exile, or a hit man tracks you down. I knew that I'd never see my friend again, and could only wish the best for her. And even though everyone in our neighborhood knew that I'd been protected, sheltered from harms way, and taught much of my strategy by Lucky, only she and I would ever know to what extent. So, with all things considered, I figured that it would be best that, some things should surely remain strictly between her and me. But most certainly, I was also in a state of amazement as I sat staring at that part of the report revealing Lucky as Regina's mother. That piece of information literally had taken my breath away. It was the explanation for Regina's education, clout within the city, and her hustler awareness. Also, it helped me to explain why her exceptional poise and beauty had struck me as so familiar.

CHAPTER SEVENTEEN

Seven O'clock came and I was headed for the big meeting. When I arrived, Bert's limousine was parked in the lot of the building. The office complex was in an upscale well-kept neighborhood, a total opposite from our ghetto land. As I entered the office suite, Regina greeted me, "I hope you're doing well, Jason."

"I'm doing fine, thank you."

Sitting on a leather lounge chair, from across the room, Bert said, "Come on in man, it's time to sort out your agenda."

Regina offered me a seat at her desk next to Bert, and said, "Your figures look great, but some of your ideas have strong organized crime relations, and some of them makes it seem like you're on a vendetta against white people. I'd like to hear your response to that. Plus, I'd also like for you to tell me what is going to stop someone from killing you?"

"Very good questions," I said. "Direct and to the point. As far as the criminal element goes, I'm really not going to cut anyone out of the deal that is already in the mix. Their payments will be made as already agreed. We don't want to lose the businesses of our organized crime relations; we want their participation and their connections, but not their negative influence over our communities. My proposals are merely a step towards creating a village community that benefits the good people in our area. And the part of your question about someone killing me, that's not a concern, at least not to me. You see, I'm on a mission that will carry it's own protection."

"Well, now, that's very spiritual Mr. Phillips, but what does it translate into with investors? I need a promise to take to the bargaining table, not the gospel."

She almost made me feel as if I were under attack. I said, "Your concerns are valid, but I can't give you any promises. Please Regina, don't carry me in a circle, we all know what time it is. The affiliation between you and Bert alone can knock down any wall that's in front of me right now, and we all know it. You and I have both checked up on each other, so let's stop playing games, and take care of business."

She looked at Bert as he nodded in acceptance of what I was trying to say, then surprisingly, said, "Please continue as if I'd already made the decision to back you."

"Thank you." Then I turned to face them both and proceeded to re-address the issue at hand. "This town is cut in half. One set of people control the north side, and the south side belongs to us. Fortunately, the cash flow is great in both areas. But unfortunately, none of it seems to be fluid enough to come back and fund a restoration of our community. This situation has caused a corruption that has flooded our way of living with a state of poverty. Please, allow me to explain."

From the files on my desk, I held up the charts I'd screened of the areas that Bert controlled, and continued, "Please follow the marked areas. Before any progress can be made in any of these areas, a general house cleaning has to be done. We will make direct attacks on the slumlords, food and merchandise price-fixers, as well as those loan-sharking pawnbrokers; they will all have to find a new place to do business. These are just a few of the vultures that I intend to rid our neighborhoods of. Our organization, if we can form one, will control the new businesses that we'll create from within. The money generated by those businesses will fund the rebuilding of the village format that we know once existed. Do y'all follow me?"

They both confirmed that they understood my direction, but Regina said, "I've got a feeling that this can work, but only if you've got the guts to remain honest, and alive, during what's going to be a process of changing the mind sets of people."

I sensed a concern for my well being in her voice. It was refreshing when I began to feel that she had a caring heart to match her outside beauty. She stood and said, "This project seems to be more than just another money making operation, and we may even be able to create a climate that can reeducate our people on how to live. Although money must be made, maybe also, we can be proud of this project. I'm going to give you a green light. Take this deal as a nucleus and let's try on your restructure concept for size. We'll see how it fits."

Bert stood, smiling as he said, "Sounds like you need to get busy J.P. But remember this, when you ask me to do something for you, don't forget my style. If you need a mule to plow your fields, be prepared to deal with the mess that I'm, I mean, he is gonna make."

I stood up and gave my buddy some Dap, and said, "I understand brother. Let's just do this."

Regina witnessed our handshake routine and said, "How do you close a deal with a female partner?"

She caught me totally off my guard. Although to me, it sounded like she wanted me to make a pass at her. So, I smoothly said, "I really would like to take you out for dinner. I'd truly welcome the chance to get to know you as a person, as well as a partner."

"For now," she said. "All either of us need to do is to understand the partner. If your plan is solid, we can do business whether I like you or not, but I am hungry. Meetings adjourned, let's eat."

Bert turned toward me, teasing me about the weak rap I'd just used on Regina, and said, "I guess that will cool off the playboy, in the homeboy. But since my name wasn't mentioned in the food conversation, guess I must not be hungry. But, it's all good, all in fun, partners. Anyway, we all know I've got plenty of business that needs handling?"

I said, "Thanks again for your support man, but before the night is over, I'd like for you to talk with Archie. Earlier today, he and I discussed some restructuring plans that I'd like you to know about. I also explained to him that you're the one he'll be dealing with."

"That was a good move J. It's good to see you ahead of the game. I'll stop by the Ritz later and see what's up."

For a fine place to dine, Regina and I only had to go to the top floor of her office building. The complex housed a four star restaurant that offered great steaks, and a scenic view of the city from ten floors high. As we were seated, my emotions began to surge with excitement. Being in the company of Regina was becoming a pleasant experience.

The waiter arrived and said, "Good evening Miss Mallory. Are you and your guest ready to order?"

Graciously she replied, "Yes Tony, I think I'll have my usual lobster and shrimp dish please, and water will be fine to drink."

Turning to me, he said, "And you sir, what would like?"

"I think I'll just have a salad, with a side order of your top sirloin, and a stuffed baked potato."

Politely, the accommodating waiter smiled and said, "Certainly Sir. " Then to Regina, "Your dinner will be served shortly, Miss Mallory."

As the waiter left, Regina looked at me, and said, "Why the jive talk Jason?"

I smiled and said, "I was hoping to break the ice of formality between you and me. Taking care of business is what I do, but that's not who I am. I've already figured that you and I are going to be great partners, now I'm hoping that we can start to become friends."

I got a smile from her, and then she said, "I heard that you had a good sense of humor. It's good to know that I won't have to deal with that stone face of yours all of the time."

We shared in a laugh together over her comment, and during the course of dinning, only talked of things that the two of us found to be enjoyable. I could almost sense the air of compatibility between the two of us. Momentarily, I even imagined what a fine mother she would make for a son of mine. But, she quickly brought my thoughts back to reality. She said, "Jason, I'm going to tell you the truth about why I'm giving your concept my support. When I told you that yours was not a new concept, I was literally telling you that you're not alone with your dream. Others feel and share in your vision of a village concept."

Attentively, I listened as she went on to tell me that there were some original plans for Memphis. The city's black leaders had planned to use Memphis as a testing ground for the development of an area that would offer black people a quality standard for living. She informed me that those plans had never been abandoned. The original group of planners for the project suffered set backs with their plan because of a lack of leadership and corruption in society. Leaders had been paid off, shot, jailed, or simply run out of town under threats from bogus arrest warrants that had been issued against them by crooked law enforcers. Once the cheaters had dismantled the core of guidance, money that had been allocated to maintain and develop our communities was left to be divided between the greedy jackals and selfish amongst black people. The original groups of planners, known as the OGP, were made up from the moral up-standing people within our community, who also worked hand and glove with the leaders that were in the underworld. In reality, the mix and the OGP were one in the same. Regina continued, and said; "We've known our problem for some time now. We've got money and connections to make almost anything possible. In my opinion, the only thing that has been slowing us down is that we need someone with a vision, someone that we can trust. Members of the OGP trust you, Jason, they think of you as family, and they were waiting to see if you would see our circumstance and make an attempt to put the pieces of our puzzle together on your own. We are all pleased that you made the first step. So, I say work your vision, and we'll stand by you until the bitter end. It's like Bert said, "You the man." But, I promise you that if you run a con game on our people, I will personally take you out, and that's a matter of fact."

Earnestly, I looked at Regina and said, "You asked me for a promise to take to the bargaining table. Win lose or draw, I promise you that Memphis won't be the same when I'm finished."

After a great meal, with the best of company, I drove from that office complex on the outskirts of town and returned home, back to ghetto land. As much as I would've liked for things to be different, but due to our dilemma, months would pass before another opportunity for Regina and I would be able to share any personal time together again. Although, as the days and weeks passed, time finally came when I had all of my ducks in a row. All of the necessary components for our organization were in place and I decided that we should share our ghetto experience with the north side residents. The north side was where those, dog politicians, lived that had allowed drugs to be routed through our neighborhoods. It was also where the representatives of financial institutions lived. With their discriminating lending policies, they'd done just as much damage to our areas as any other had. They all literally foamed at the mouth like rabid beasts, from their anticipation of the profits that could be made from our black population. But, I was about to give all of those buzzards a taste of what it was like to have your situation disturbed. As a strategy, I delegated the disruption of the affluent north side residents to Bert. Under his direction, it was to be arranged for all of our local hood-rats to be transported daily too cumbersome points north of Beale Street. Bums, derelicts, wine drinkers, and hoodlums, would be released to create havoc in those affluent communities. They were instructed to vandalize, disrupt the peace, sell dope, shoplift, and whatever else they could think of that would cause the police to focus their attention on that side of town. When the members of that rascal team that were arrested, they'd be bailed out the next day by Homer. He'd use the money that had been made from the overall ante of the team's take. For those on the team that didn't get nabbed, they were picked up each morning by our drivers and later returned for more mayhem. At the same time that these disturbances by our rat pack would be taking place, Archie and his crew would be on their mission to harass the businesses of the blue light track area. I wanted to completely disrupt normal business proceedings and the living conditions of all those that we had targeted. Eventually, the whole town would be in an uproar, demanding public officials to take action against the disturbances that our implants would be causing.

To cause problems for our blue light district, Archie had his team in tact and they were sitting on ready. But, my man Bert needed a couple of good hands from the street that we could trust. To get our desired affect, I knew exactly whom we needed, and where to find them. I drove to Buck George's liquor store to track down my two thug buddies, Jake and Zak. When I cruised up on to the store's lot, there they were. Zak was first to see me.

"J. P.! What's the word, good buddy? Come over here and give a brother five. Look Jake, its J.P!"

I got out of my car as they both came over to greet me. Casually I said, "Looks like the same game with you two fellows. Long as I been gone, it still seems like y'all ain't gonna do nothing but party for the rest of your lives."

Jake replied, in an intoxicated stupor, "You got that right, man. But now, we be doing it to the bone. See man, now we got them hippie type white boys paying for the party. They be giving us good dope to sell, and it's all on credit. You want a toot?

Quickly, I said, "No, I've got things to do, brothers." For a while, we continued to joke and jive, but then I said, "You bean-heads must have not been keeping up with the news, have you?"

Jake pranced in a circle, and babbled, "We got all the news we needs to know 'bout. We know we got plenty of money, plenty of high, and it's all good. But it's still good to see you again, man. Tell us what we been missing?"

I announced, "I'm gonna clean up our town. Ain't gonna stop nobody from doing what they do, but you just might have to change your hangout, and who you'll be spending your money with. That's about all it is to it."

Zak said, "I don't mind that. You don't either, do you Jake?"

Jake gave a sigh of indifference, as he said, "Same game, new players, don't matter none to me, just as long as don't nobody go up on the price of the toot. Me, man I really don't like them hillbillies we been dealing with anyway."

Straightforward and point blank, I said to my two junky buddies, "Listen up for a minute. I need to pull some new tricks on the man, but I ain't playing no games. Can I still trust you two ding-dongs?"

Jake took another sip from his bottle of wine, and said, "If you got a plan, we'll work with you. But, we can't commit to no lost and found operation. We might not be making money like gangbusters, but we doing ok. We be selling twenty cent smack capsules, dime rocks of crack, nickel hits of speed, and dollar joints. Them be our customers. So, whatever game you wanna play on the man, just don't be messing up our money."

Impatiently, I said, "Sounds like you two dip sticks are playing with me, but you need to catch this boat before it sails. Things are about to change, and I'm not really asking you two-bit hustlers for approval. I need somebody that I can trust. The money is gonna be good and you'll stay supplied. Now you tell me, what time is it?"

Zak stepped to the forefront and assuredly said, "J., that boy is speaking through his nose, but I speak for the both of us cause my brain ain't fried yet. You know that you can count on both of us for whatever you need. Word up, big Jake?"

With his head held down, Jake said, " J., I wasn't thinking. I think I been hanging around too many crooks, you know what I mean. Zak, he be right. He speaking for me too, man. You can trust, we'll work with you."

Giving up a high-five to the two of them, I said, "Now that's the set of homeboys that I remember. So, listen up, this is the deal. Bert is gonna be in touch with you in a couple of days, and I want y'all to follow his lead, even if it sounds a little strange. Y'all might end up spending a little time in jail, but don't give up on me. I can't tell y'all everything, that's why I need people that I can trust, and that trust me. If y'all just follow Bert's lead, we'll all be in good shape."

With a grin, Zak said, "Well, both of us done been in jail before, and it ain't nothing but a thang, just like a turkey wang."

Jake and Zak might have been worthless to the rest of the world, but they were a made to order pair for the needs of our project. After a couple of weeks of them working their special magic, the newspaper's headlines read; "Crime on the north side, rapidly on the rise." Those citizens, and the people of the blue light area, all had registered complaints, demanding for public officials to take some kind of action. And in the midst of the melee, our plans forged ahead, blue prints were drafted for building our new beginning. Even Reverend Clark had started to announce the joyful news that structural and moral changes were about to be implemented. The blue prints for our villages were mapped out to favor our upright citizens of the community, and those who chose to live an alternative way. The rough draft of our neighborhood was for the new blue light district to be located on the east side of town, and that would be the only area for underworld activities to operate in. Bert and Archie's army would ensure that. Since the west side of town was the most beautiful part of the city, bordered by the river, it was designed for our new village community's way of life, off limits to immoral street activities. Our people would learn, grow, and make that area a place worthy of calling home

Chapter Eighteen

"Ring, ring, ring. Hello."

"Good morning, Jason,"

"Hi Regina, how is my favorite partner doing?"

"I'm fine. I got our first reaction from the city officials this morning."

"Were they referencing the newspaper headline?"

"Yes, they sure were."

"Well, tell me, where do we stand?"

"We've got their attention," she said. "They called me wanting to know what was going on, and who was responsible. Two district commissioners, a representative from the Mayor's office, and one from the sheriff's department, they all want to arrange a meeting with me."

"That's great, just what we wanted. Are you prepared to handle it?"

"Yes, but do you understand just how important this meeting is going to be? This will be one of the most crucial factors towards our progress."

"I agree with you. This meeting is important and I'm ready."

With a hint of uncertainty in her voice, she said, "I scheduled the meeting for tomorrow night, but I think that you and I need to go over our agenda before I see them. We need to make sure that we're both on the same page."

"I agree, just tell me what's easy for you?"

She asked, "Can you come to my house around noon today?"

In spite of my attraction for Regina, we had maintained a strictly business relationship with each other. I was pleased with our progress, but I had become curious about seeing how this special lady lived her life away from the public. Pleased with her invitation, I said, "That'll be fine, the sooner we can meet, the better. The faster we can get our intentions across to those city officials, the faster we can move ahead."

Also to my pleasure, she surprisingly said, "Bring an appetite, I'll fix us some lunch."

Happily, I said, "That sounds great, see you at noon."

On the way to Regina's house, driving from our neighborhood to hers was like leaving a junkyard and entering the Taj Mahal. The wealthy community that she lived in was far away from the reaches of all the city's troubles. It was a segregated area, not by law, but because only a few of us had enough money to live there anyway. Briefly, I wondered whether or not Regina was going to turn out to be like those people that believed in the idea; I've got mine, now you get yours.

"Ding, dong."

"Hello Jason, please come in."

I entered into the lavish interior of her home with rubber knees and shortness of breath, accompanied by a rapid heartbeat. The irregularity was not from the beauty of her mini-mansion, but from the sight of her beauty. The very professional businesswoman now revealed her true beautiful self. The usual business attire that I was accustomed to seeing had been replaced by a pair of blue biker shorts that fit like a glove, and a blouse that exposed nothing, but showed the curves of everything. Even her neat bun hairdo was released to where her hair hung freely around her sleek and shapely shoulders. Good taste practically radiated from her, and everything that surrounded her. She led me through a corridor of her home and into a spacious contemporary living area, turned to me, and said, "Are you ready to eat, or talk first?"

I managed to avoid stuttering in my state of excitement, and said, "Let's eat."

We ate on the terrace overlooking her swimming pool, and conversed as new friends, until it felt as if we were old friends. After lunch, she said, "Would you like a drink before we get started?"

Resisting the temptation, I used my better judgment and said, "No, but thank you. Lunch was great and I've enjoyed our conversation, but we do have some important things to discuss."

She escorted me to her den and said, "Now, let's see how we want to approach tomorrow night's meeting."

"Okay. But next time, let me treat you to as nice a lunch as you've given me."

She smiled and said, "My pleasure, I'll be looking forward to it." Leading me to the den, where we took seats across from each other, separated by her marbled antique coffee table, she continued to say, "In your opinion, Jason, how would you like for me to approach the meeting with the officials?"

Still in a relaxed mood, I said, "Just tell them that a new man is in charge, here to do a job that no one else seems to want to handle."

Abruptly, she stood and momentarily paced up and down the floor, returned to her seat, took a breath, and avidly expressed, "Jason! This is the top of our action, don't take it lightly. If you don't know what to say, don't say anything! We both know how badly our people need this project to be successful, so don't make people think that I'm representing a gangster."

I sat back in my chair, and rephrased my comment, "Regina, I apologize for my lackadaisical response, but don't misunderstand. When you meet with the people downtown, let them know that we are only reestablishing our community in the best way that we know how. We want to revamp our already populated area to represent an example of prosperity for all that choose to live there."

"I'm sorry that I exploded, Jason, but I believe that you do understand my anxiety. After all, you're the one that caused me to clearly see our position, one that I've been in denial about. As well to do as I might appear, you were right in your assessment. Its true that my neighbors would rather I lived elsewhere."

"I understand Regina. On the real side, I'd like for you to make those officials understand that we won't take any money out of their pockets. But, we will take money that has normally been seized in arrest, along with other valued confiscated contraband, and what used to be a jackleg attorney's fee. Things that once depleted a dealer's capital, will now build our schools. The prostitutes, gamblers, and hustler's profits, will now offer us percentages to give our elderly housing. The city officials that you're going to meet with have not, and never will stop the vices that have existed since the beginning of time. They know that in some shape, form or fashion, vices will always exist. So, we will take advantage of some vices, and acquire capital from them for our community. With that money, we will create a place for our young people to become productive citizens, rather than just users and consumers. Let the people downtown know that they will get their cut, but we will have our way of life restored. Yet, when things are all said and done, they may still call me a gangster, hustler, con artist, thief or humanitarian, I don't know. But, I do know that, if the Lord is willing, we will be successful."

With an air of understanding, and a sigh of relief, she said, "Now that's something that I can use to blow the roof off with. Now that the ball is in my court, I can create an effective strategy."

We finished our meeting and I prepared to make my exit. As Regina opened the door for me to leave, I said, "Call me when you find out what's what. I've still got a lot left to do today, but as soon as we both find the time, I'd like to see you again. But this time, no business, okay?"

Softly, she said, "Yeah, sure Jason, I'd like that."

I left pretty Regina at the doorway waving good-bye, but not before I'd given her a thank you kiss on the cheek. Then, to keep things progressing according to schedule, I drove to Peace in Faith church to talk with Reverend Clark. When I arrived, respectfully I said, "How have you been, Sir?"

"I'm doing fine Son. Is all of that mess I've been reading in the papers because of you?"

"Yes, it is Sir. And there's plenty more to come."

"Boy, you're going to need much prayer boy."

Humbly, I said, "Yes Sir, you're right, but thanks to you, many of our good citizen's have gotten the word that our new day is coming. I'm glad that we're working toward the same goal, but I'm here because I'm going to need more help from you, as well as more prayer. Sir, I'm ready to speed things up."

"What do you need now Jason?"

Cautiously I requested, "For those that you know can handle it, I need you and them to stand at the gates of hell."

"Do what!"

"I need your group to stand at both entrances of the blue light district with your bibles and picket signs that say, Jesus saves. I want you all to sing at the top of your voices for the sinners to go home. I want to try giving guilty thoughts to as many of the district's patrons as possible. Archie and his group will insure protection for the safety of your people."

"You're really going to shut them down, aren't you?"

I paused, pondered my response, and said, "No Reverend, I'm not going to shut them down, but they will have to move. That land was made for living, and it's much too beautiful for that much sin to be allowed to continue."

"Jason, the victory for the righteous will be won. My vision shows that this is your cross to carry and your battle to fight in the name of Jesus. My congregation, and I will form a committee. Together, with you, we will walk through the valley of the shadows of death, and fear no evil. We'll help shield you, and try to supply strength for your destiny, for the sake of us all."

"Thank you Sir. And although there will be trouble in this endeavor, I can assure you that, the buck stops here. When trouble wants to start a rumble, I will stop it. No harm will ever come to any of your people."

CHAPTER NINETEEN

Our efforts caused a lot of illegal business to close their doors. That meant more money had to be generated to maintain a good standing with the city officials and other elements of organized crime. So, I made a trip to seek help from my old friend Dollar Bill, owner of the old "Hole in the Wall Bar and Grill." He had warehouse space perfectly located on the East Side, and with his approval and assistance, we were able to refurbish it. The "Hole in the Wall" was reopened and became our first new blue light district sight. That nightclub generated our organization immediate, capital. It also became a great money-laundering marketplace. Over a period of several months, all of the businesses of the old track area were forced to close. The owners and operators of those businesses began to negotiate for relocation to our new area. The old blue light district soon became a ghost town.

Regina had successfully put the city officials and other corrupt business leaders in check; things were going better than we'd anticipated. When adequate money was being generated from our own region, we contemplated the means of construction for our new West Side village community. After seeing the plans for the new development, and with approval of the organization, I asked Bert to do a different type of ground clearing. I asked my pyromaniac buddy to remember his happy lighter fluid days. In turn, he responded, and the old West Side, an already dilapidated eye sore, was burned down to the ground by unknown arsons. Then, Regina used more of her political influence to pull some strings, and although our area was a victim of unexplained arson, she had her people to report that lightening was the blame. The damage done was considered to be brought on by natural causes, an act of God, and our prime sites were declared a certified disaster area. By the time she had finished manipulating he politicians, she'd acquired federal funding and other government subsidies for us to rebuild.

Ground clearing and construction from our calculated blue prints were given the okay to get underway. Regina, Reverend Clark and I began to implement those prints for the priority of first construction. The designated boundaries of our new community were from east to west, just as preplanned. We started with the track zoning of the blue light district as our eastern borderline. The single's units and double-leveled apartment complexes would be next, with our shopping malls, grocery stores, and the specialty shops of entrepreneurs, serving as a separating junction. Our community would continue to span westward with Reverend Clark's new church as our central landmark. It would be recognized as the core of the community. Next to our new home of worship would be a fully facilitated community center, equipped with a staff qualified to offer us a twenty four hour child care program, plus youth and adult recreation. Mrs. Harden had joined forces with our group and had offered to head up and design our school system to accommodate pre-kindergarten through the twelfth grade, all from within one major compound. Our housing complexes for senior citizens would border the school grounds of our new learning institution and family dwellings would follow. The Mississippi River front would be our west border, accommodating the higher income individuals, homes for the wealthy. Those boundaries earmarked everything between Beale Street and Tennessee's southern border, marking our areas of operation to accommodate complete construction for a new community village.

During the time of development for our project, I talked to Mama, Evelyn and her family often. Mama had decided to stay with Evelyn because I was doing so well with my new, real estate company. She had also read of the improvements in the city and knew that I was a key element in its refurbishing. Mama was very proud of me, and what she knew about was very true; she just didn't know the whole story. However, I did let her know that I'd become involved with a lady that I respected and liked very much, and that her name was Regina.

Time went on, and after a couple of years had passed, our project brought many rewards, in spite of the many difficulties. One night as I rested, I began to ponder the success of our group's accomplishments against the odds that we had faced. Many bribes of under the table deals had been offered, but rejected. All sorts of threats had been made and plenty of legal battles were fought, and they had all been overcome. As different as our team was in our own unique personalities, the bond of wanting to change our people's lifestyle had repelled our foe's every effort to divide us. Each administrative member controlled their areas according to that individual's expertise, and I began to feel that I'd become the businessman of my dreams. But it was soon to be a dream that was abruptly disturbed.

"Ring, ring, ring. "Hello."

"Get out of the house, J.! This Homer, man. They gonna blow you away!"

"Bang, bang, bang!"

I dropped to the floor with my heart pounding and quickly low-crawled down the stairs to the front door. I don't recall if there had been six shots fired, or twenty-six. I was frightened as I opened the door looking for a getaway. Then suddenly, in disgust, I moaned at the sight I witnessed. "Ahea man, no. What happened?"

Three bullet riddled bodies lay mangled and twisted in a sea of blood on my front lawn, with Bert standing over them, a smoking forty-five automatic in each of his hands. He blew smoke from the pistol barrels, and said, "You okay buddy?"

I jumped over the aftermath of his action and ran to him with a wide-eyed hysteria, "Homer said someone was 'bout to blow me away."

With a stare as cold as an iceberg, from eyes that were gleaming like black diamonds, he looked at me and calmly said, "He called me first."

Confused and still in a state of shock, I asked, "What we gonna do man?"

Quick he responded, "I've done my job. You the man, next move, that be your call."

Enraged, I shouted, "Get real Bert! You just gunned down three people."

Putting me in check, he replied, "Get real yourself, and stop shouting. This ain't the first bunch that had to go down to make stuff work around here. I ain't been asking how you make things work and you ain't been asking me. Now, sho-nuff ain't the time to start. I just did what I been doing all along, keeping the peace and keeping you alive. Handle your business, J."

Calming down, I said, "Bert, I can't just play this off."

Conveniently he reminded me, "Remember what I told you? If you use a mule to plow your fields, be prepared to handle his mess. I gotta roll partner. Later."

With screeching tires, Bert drove away, as I viewed his work. Glad to be alive, I went into the house and called 911. "There has been a drive by shooting in front of my house. Could you please send an ambulance?"

I managed to regain my composure enough to answer the police questions when they arrived. Since I didn't really have much information to offer them, I wasn't detained. But, after the police completed their investigation, and I was alone, a spirit of remorse blanketed my mind. Surely, I knew that Mama wouldn't be very proud of many of the things that I'd done. And, I dared not look into a mirror. The price that I had been charged to spearhead the progress for black people in Memphis had been for me to sacrifice some parts of my moral concepts and me. I'd been willing to pay any price to achieve my goal, but not at the cost of my soul. I jumped into my car and drove to Peace in Faith. When I arrived, I fell to my knees at the altar, and prayed. This time it wasn't for discernment, but for the forgiveness of my sins.

For a few days, I reviewed the hit men's attempt on my life and analyzed the changes that had formed in my attitude. I realized that my compassion for the emotional needs, and the basic concerns of many people had taken a back seat to my aggressiveness toward success in the OGP's endeavors. The death of the three people that I knew about, and the harm that I'm sure had to have happened to many others, didn't really matter very much to me. I'd become callous. My intentions had been all good and my efforts had produced positive results, but my inner rage against the cheaters that were guilty of racial atrocities had collided with my productive and assertive mannerisms. That rage had ushered its way into the personality of my character. I was a leader with the mentality of a warrior that had been trained to believe that to a hammer, everything is a nail. I believed that power never would be relinquished without a fight, and I'd hammered away at whatever got in the way of expedient progress. With collaborated forces, I had power, but little tact, and less diplomacy. But, Regina was my stabilizing force, my diplomat, and the only person I believed understood my heart. She was an intellectual negotiator, with independent thoughts that seemed to merge perfectly in teaching me a lesson on compassion for others. Subtlety, she taught me the importance of never forgetting the human touch. She and I had begun a relationship of togetherness that depicted each of our dreams as one. Even in my stubbornness, I always listened to her. Yet, arrogantly I'd flaunt her as my prize, and coined her as my queen. Then, I realized that Regina had become more important to me than the reality of our new community. At the height of my inconsiderate ways of being, it was her that set the actions of my personality characteristics back on the road of my heart's original intentions. She showed me the extent of my Neanderthal, caveman like behavior. She let me know, in her diplomatic way, that a cold-hearted manner of being wouldn't be acceptable to her. In her doing so, she also opened a door that allowed me to discover a major revelation about myself.

One summer's night, Regina and I spent a beautiful evening on a riverboat excursion on the Mississippi River. It was a formal affair on a very special riverboat vessel. The craft was a luxury steamboat, a replica of the once renowned Mississippi gamblers of old, reminiscent of the Mark Twain era. For the full flavor of a formal evening out, it was accented with antique furnishings of that era, hulls of ivory and trimmed in gold. The steam-forced, paddle-propelled cruiser majestically sparkled in the night from the moon's glowing reflections. It was a true work of art, a tourist attraction that our city took great pride in. Known as the river's finest craft, she was royally named as the Mississippi's floating queen, "The Leeondrya."

We had a fine time on that first class riverboat, and after "The Leeondrya" docked, we went to Regina's place for some quiet time alone. When we arrived she went into the bedroom to make herself a bit more comfortable. I went into the den and prepared us some refreshments. While waiting for her to return, I set the stereo to play some soothing music and began to relax on the sofa, sipping my wine and enjoying a good Havana cigar. As I was relaxing, I noticed her wide-eyed jet-black Persian cat. I had seen the feline many times before, but he had always maintained his distance from me. For some reason, this night was different; he attempted to approach me. I don't know if it was the alcohol or what, but as the cat neared, I began to imagine it as a stalker of the jungle. The creature crept over a chair and around the table, maneuvering his way to the edge of the sofa where I sat. Now, somewhat mesmerized by it's graceful movements, I found myself sitting back and trying to make eye to eye contact by staring the beast down. But, the stalker paused, and returned my stare. Then, in one smooth leap, he jumped to the head of the sofa and slowly walked towards me. When he strutted directly up to me, instead of me rewarding him for his friendly efforts, I received him with a childish prank. I exhaled a puff of imported cigar smoke, right into his face. Instantly, he darted from the room, leaving me with a bad boy's smirk on my face. But just as luck would have it, Regina was standing in the doorway. Angrily, she said, "I certainly hope that you're not proud of that display of crude insensitivity that I just witnessed."

What could I have said? What could I have done? I'd been cold-busted. Actually, I felt reminiscent of my younger days, when that bull elephant at the zoo used me for his Kleenex. Yet, slightly unconcerned, I looked at her and said, "Ah, baby, I was just having some fun. I didn't mean to hurt the little fellow."

She turned to me with a sad and angry face as she said, "I'm sure Lang didn't see the humor in your tasteless joke, and neither did I. Don't you know that I love my pet? He's been a great comfort to me, and you should respect that; At least enough not to purposely annoy him!"

I walked toward her with my arms extended to embrace her, and said, "Let's not make a mountain out of such a small thing."

Abruptly, she turned and quickly left the room. I followed her as she ran into the bedroom and lay across the bed with tear filled eyes. Momentarily, I stopped and stood in the doorway, baffled. I didn't even realize what I had done, didn't have a clue as to how important that incident was to her. Then, it finally dawned on me that I'd actually hurt her. That night, I learned that you must continually be conscious of making your loved one happy, because the affairs of the heart are never mastered. I also learned that consideration was a major ingredient in the recipe of life. With my newfound awareness, softly I tried to speak to her from the bedroom's entrance. I humbled myself and said, "Ignorance of the law is never an excuse for a crime, and I won't use it for a reason, or an excuse. Regina, I sincerely ask your forgiveness, and I want you to know that your tears are felt by me. In my mind, hurting you is a criminal act. It doesn't even really matter whether or not I know how or why you're hurt, just knowing that you're hurt is enough to bring that same pain to me. I'm human, baby, and I will make mistakes. But, when that does happen, I want you to know that my intentions are good. I may unintentionally cause you some sadness, but I guarantee you that for each time that I do, I will also purposely try to replace that sadness with gladness. I love you Regina, for all that you are, and for all that you'll ever become. If you can just find room in your heart to take a chance on me, if you would just allow me to enrich my heart with the love that I feel exists between the two of us; my life is yours to love. And, I would very much like for your life to be for me to love."

She listened to me from across the bedroom with her face turned away. But, when I'd finished talking, she rewarded me with the attention of her sweet delicate brown eyes. Then, she slowly arose and sat at the edge of the bed, extending a hand in invitation. I walked to her bedside and gently caressed it, as she said, "Jason, I know what you've been, and I know what you've become. I also know what you can be. I know too, that you're a very easy man to love. But, this is what I need to know about you. I need to know whether or not you can love. You know that I have a choice from the group of men who love me, but that really does-n't matter because I don't love any of them. I am what I am, and I have to believe that I'm loved for that, and that alone. But, a chance for you to love me, and for me to love you, that's a chance worth taking. So, you just go right ahead and feel free to continue being that unshakable piece of granite stone to the world. But, when you come to me, just try a little tenderness."

With an enlightened frame of mind, tenderly we embraced each other and kissed, sealing a bond that both of us had longed for. From that day on, we both knew that whatever else might happen in our futures, we both would always know the joy of loving, and being loved in return. Our feelings brought together a union of our bodies, a union that gave me my first experience of not just having an affair with a lady for the sake of merely the affair. I made love with someone that I loved for the first time that night, and with someone who loved me. I loved the feeling of our togetherness, as we formed into a unity that could someday equal the total of one.

CHAPTER TWENTY

Seasons changed as time went by, and the OGP diligently continued to drive toward the completion of rebuilding our community until our dream finally becomes a reality. On one joyful Sunday morning, I received my heart's reward. That day, I sat in church and listened to Reverend Clark deliver a very special announcement. Proudly, he announced, "Today, we acknowledge the works done through the grace of our God. We have been truly blessed with the restoration of a foundation on which to build our cultural heritage. Over the span of the last several years, we all have been witnesses to the seeds that have been planted. Now, our village has begun to produce its expected crop, and we're able to reap a sweeter fruit. Better jobs are more plentiful, and our neighborhoods are both, cleaner and safer for everybody. On this day, our entity is within the framework of one nation under our Lord."

On that day, a proud and happy congregation of Americans born of African heritage was dismissed from our new house of worship. It was a special feeling for me to see such a promising future ahead us. The members of our organization had done their jobs very well, and progress was evident, in spite of the resistance. Many people in power had tons of dirt on our organization, enough to legally jail most of our staff, but thanks to Regina, we had just as much dirt on them. Her information helped us to balance the scales at the bargaining tables, and her political dirt was concrete and irrefutable. Consequently, instead of diverse groups from around the city tossing malicious dirt to soil each other, or us, we all learned to coexist and wash our own dirty laundry. It was because of this that the OGP was confident and secure in the majority of our political and underworld dealings. But, there was another problem that needed to be addressed. Black people needed to be taught how to regain their sense of pride. The mental damage from the many years of racism had dampened the spirits of too many. Our people's minds were the areas that had been affected most by our travails. Black people in Memphis needed to realistically look at the games that had been played on us in the past. So in search of answers, a few days later, I headed back to Peace in Faith to discus a direction with the reverend. But, on my way to the church, I decided to take a quick inspection of the conditions of the blue light district. Surprisingly, I found Jake sitting under a bridge, crying. I rolled down the window and called him over to the car. "What's up with you dude? Your stash done got low? Are you out of high, or what?"

He continued to sit, crouched over and weeping like a newborn baby. Impatiently, I shouted. "Don't just sit there like a knot on a log. Man, say something?"

Suddenly, Jake screamed. "They done killed him J.P.! They done killed him! It's Zak. He dead man."

I immediately got out of the car and ran over to him. "What's up man? Straighten yourself up and tell me what you're talking about."

Slowly he stood to his feet, and with head and eyes pointed to the ground, said, "Zak, man, he dead."

With a sunken heart, I said, "Ain't y'all been under Bert's control? He's been giving me good reports on the both of you. What, how, tell me something? Stop crying man and tell me what happened."

"J., we was on our way home when the cops stopped us. I jumped out the car and ran. But Zak, he was driving, they got him. They arrested him, man. He wasn't in that jail for three hours before someone opened his throat with a razor."

"Why didn't you try to call somebody after you got away? How come you didn't contact Homer?"

"I didn't have time to call Homer, Bert or nobody else. Junior Jones, he was down at the jail visiting his brother when it happened. His brother told him that thangs happened so fast, it seemed like they killed Zak before he got in the cell good. He said that it was one of those, alien Aryan nation skinhead kind of folks that did it."

"Jake, why did the police stop y'all?"

"I think we was set up, man."

"Who wanted to set y'all up, and why?"

"You see, I think it was some white boys. Me and Zak, we went across town and made a deal with them 'bout some smack and crack, but before we left, Zak, he started to play with one of they ladies. I believe that pissed them off. I kind of heard one of them say they was gonna give Zak some payback. But since him and me could've whooped up on all of them suckers, what they said didn't phase me none. J., I think they called the law on us after we left, because on our way home, all of a sudden the police just stopped us for nothing."

I broke into a frantic rage. "Man, both y'all dumb!" "You telling me that Zak got whacked over a hit of crack, a snort of smack, and a two-dollar piece of snatch? Jake, Brother Zak and you were wrong. Ain't nothing left now but to try and save you from making the same selfish mistake. Next time it could be you, and I've already lost enough brothers. Man, why couldn't y'all stay within our new laws, what went wrong?"

"J., me and old Zak, we just wanted to get some high and have a little fun with the chicks. We were just trying to have a good time. You know what I mean."

"Jake, you need much help, you're a sick man. The OGP has made things better for us, but we don't allow our people to get lazy and crazy. Can't any of us forget about the folks that still live, and want us dead. You know that it's plenty of folks out there that don't want us to make no progress. You! You listen up, Jake. Get some help. Go see Reverend Clark."

Stupidly, he replied, "I don't know 'bout that J. The Rev., he can't help me, ain't no such thang as miracles."

"Wake up bonehead! Do what I asked you to do. What do you mean, ain't no such thing as miracles? You're still breathing, ain't you? That should be all the proof of miracles that you need."

After such an emotionally heartbreaking experience, I knew for sure, a matter of such importance as us understanding ourselves as responsible black men and women had to be addressed by the OGP. In the chain of our organization's command, the decisions really came down to Regina, Bert, and me. However, when I asked them for ideas on ways to help rejuvenate the self-pride that was hidden inside of our people, both of them were quick to inform me of my position from within the OGP's command chain. I visited Regina first, and she explained, "Jason, my area of expertise is in handling the political arena. I understand the extent of the mind pollution among our people, but really, I don't know how we can effectively approach the problem. Although, as I recall, you're the one that's supposed to put the pieces of this puzzle together, and make them fit."

I was somewhat disappointed and wanted someone to give me some answers. But, considering her response, I just said, "Yeah, I do recall saying that."

Next, I went to see Bert and explained the dilemma to him. "Okay old buddy, Regina has waived her input on this one. You got any ideas?"

"Not unless somebody starts some trouble. Everything else that happens, that's your business J. Do what you're supposed to be good at; put the pieces together and make them fit. That's what you need to do. Handle it."

Disgusted, I said, "Yeah, guess I'll just have to waive your vote, too. How 'bout that?"

In spite of not getting help from Bert, we still gave up our Dap handshake before I left, and he said, "I know that's important stuff you dealing with buddy. I know cause I gotta deal with the worst of those nut-buckets everyday. But, just like every thing else, you'll get it under control."

I responded to his understanding of our problem, and his trust in me, "Thanks, man. I'll catch you on the rebound. Later, brother."

After talking with my two partners, I assumed the responsibility of finding a method of remedy. Considering that both of them had conveniently reminded me of something that I'd once said, I thought that I'd do the same thing to someone else. Bingo!

"Ring, ring, ring. Hello."

"Hello, Mrs. Harden, this is Jason. May I please come over and talk to you?"

"Sure Jason, come anytime you like. I'll be home all day."

"Thanks Mrs. Harden. I'll see you in about thirty minuets."

A relief came over me when she obligingly said, "Okay son, I'll be here."

I went to her because I'd remembered what she'd said when I asked her about the colors of our high school's flag, and also when she convinced me to enroll at Chelsea. She'd said, "Jason, you still know how to listen to your heart. One day in your time of need, and at a stage of liberation, there will be an alumnus waiting to assist you in your venture."

When I arrived at Mrs. Harden's home, she immediately sensed my state of anxiety and calmed me with a cup of hot apple cider. As I sipped, I requested her assistance at this most needed time. Comfortingly, she shared her view. "It is natural for an aggressive man to become frustrated when success is slowed by a problem that has no definite solution. That's the nature of the beast. You've done an excellent job in presenting opportunities for Black people in our area, but you can't take the responsibility for them not taking advantage of those opportunities. You can take a horse to water, but you can't make him drink. As much as you and I would like to solve all of the problems faced by our brothers and sisters, we can't solve them all. Unfortunately, too many of them are self-inflicted. The only direction that can offer the highest percentages for success is the one that will unlock the doors that have imprisoned the knowledge of us as a race of people. That knowledge has been taken away from us, but it is accessible. Although, I'm really not sure if we, as a race of people, still have a thirst for the knowledge of something that we've never fully experienced. In spite of those facts, all that want a resolve for our dilemma still must find ways of restoring our people's spiritual standards of existence. All I can do is offer a message to our people, and hopefully it will enlighten some minds for some constructive changes. If you give me a platform, I'll share my knowledge. Maybe awareness can help us rid ourselves of some of the many bad habits that we've acquired. It might just give us a new direction for a method of correction. Anyway, I'm willing to try."

Respectfully I said, "Thank you Mrs. Harden."

Quick and in a hurry, I immediately put the word on the wire. "Attention, Town hall meeting; an open house is called for all village community residents, business owner's-operators, young adults, and children. Your presence is expected."

The town hall meeting was held at the community center, and to my delight, all came. As the attendance expanded to the outside grounds, we installed outside viewing screens and speakers because I wanted everybody to hear what Mrs. Harden would have to say. Then, inside the pavilion, Reverend Clark delivered her introduction. He took center stage, and announced, "In the name of Jesus Christ, our Lord and savior, we give praise and thanks to God. To gain knowledge is our responsibility for today's existence, and we must become responsible for the longevity of our village community, maintaining a consistency that promotes its good will. As a people, we have been hit mighty hard by the workings of evil, but we are still charged to stop our people's nonproductive cycle. Each of you are called here today for us to let you know how to say, no more to things that threaten our lives and souls. This is the topic to be addressed in this forum today. Ladies and gentleman, young adults, boys and girls, I proudly present to you our own minister of education, Mrs. Ella Mae Harden."

CHAPTER TWENTY-ONE

Our minister of education approached the podium and started to re-educate, in her own expedient and special way. An aura of pride and motherly love seemed to be draped around her, as she began to address the needs of the Black Americans that lived in Memphis. Powerfully, she orated, "All of you that are born on this American soil with descendants of African heritage, we are gathered here to join together in an effort to restore a harmonious unity among us. Over the years we have proven to be very durable people. God has allowed us to endure the whips, chains, and con games of our oppressors. Even their hangman's noose didn't stop us. As we experience the upgraded conditions of our community, I want us all to take full advantage of these new opportunities. Let's savor the taste of our satisfaction. We are not underdogs any longer. But, now that we have restored our own community, the time has come for us to address the mental damage that has been suffered by our people. It has taken its toll on our majority, stopping many of us from ever reaching our dreams potential. The perverted mentality of being inferior that has been perpetrated on us cannot be ignored any longer. As a race of people, we have come a long way, but a lot of us have been duped into becoming comedians of life, pranksters, and only a mere joke for the entertainment of others who actually would fear us in our true, original, spiritual nature. All too many of our unique, and creative winners, have been conned into assuming themselves as natural born losers, dictated by a media that has viewed them through a pair of cheap, three dimensional glasses. But, in true testimony of our characters, we are still here, and we're worthy contenders for the king's thrown, no longer to be the court jesters. Black people, this is your wake up call. God has given us the ability to help each other, and that's good news to share, because when it comes to us, nobody else really cares. Throughout my research for those that might assist in the plight of the black man, most of our cries have been directed to the place of our birth, America the beautiful. Many of our leaders have demanded equality from her, a square deal. America has responded, she says, "no deal." Understand me when I say that we must cure our own ills. We can no longer settle for the doses of non- effective placebos that have been given to us. If you can remember, the last bitter pill that we were asked to swallow came from our government. It festered into a housing bill that created insurance red lining. To sum things up, all of our responses for assistance from America, and around the globe, have been similar; "Do it yourself." In the spirit of truth, our young people will have to develop methods of achieving in a manner that will accommodate those responses. We have to answer our own, SOS distress call.

The concept of self-preservation has to be taught as our basics for a solid foundation. We must start with our individual selves, a mental reorientation for a forward evolution. Our calls for distress can only be answered in the acknowledgment of our self worth. Learn that you must have more to live for than that all mighty dollar bill. I caution you to understand that money is representative of gold and other precious metals, fine stones and quality minerals, which is the same stuff that false idols of biblical times were made of. Considering the fact that today we don't have an abundance of gold or other precious materials to make a golden idol to worship, too many still seem to have a burning and selfish desire for its representative. Too many people are idol worshiping, praying that they get paid. That's a serious concern that we must monitor. But, let us always remember what the inscription on our currency says. "In God we trust," and not, in the buck we trust. The addiction for money has made mankind sink mighty low, and I'd like one point to be clearly understood by black people. You can't put a price on everything, and some things are not for sale. There is not a price for your soul to be sold. There is no cash amount on how much it'll take for you to turn your back on your brother. You cannot put a price on what it will cost for you to take a life. If the brother that was killed yesterday would've lived, he may have been your best friend tomorrow. But, because of one of his own kind, that brother will never be able to watch your back.

Stop killing each other! Don't let yourselves be guilty of taking away any more lives with your bad behavior. As a culture of people, we already have to limp on a broken crutch for support to make it through everyday living. In our community, we want to make a vow that the last king has already died from the hands of the misguided. No more will die because of one of his ignorant brothers. Find someone else, other than your brother, to pick your fights with. Fight against the ones that have turned a man that once wore a crown, into a man that acts like a clown. A clown that gradually commits suicide, getting high on dope, as he watches his loved ones die along with him. Junkies! You know that it's killing your loved ones to watch you self-destruct.

People representative of all nations have shown a dislike for those of an African Heritage, and they've been guilty of many atrocities against us. Yet, through it all, we've forgiven them all. But it's time now for us to forgive each other; we must operate under a code of unity, and reinforce it by encompassing a restored sense of pride. The time is long overdue. Remember that life is beautiful, and love is the prize achievement. It's a treasure that can never be taken away from you at the whims of another. The Lord is our shepherd, and no one else shall lead us, even as the lowly sinners that we are. In our minds, as witness to those that take notice of us, we are God's representatives, and should stand tall. We can't wait for legislation to force prayer back into the schools, nor teach an understanding of the Lord to our children. Parents, I say that we must return Jesus back to our own hearts, so that we can teach our children how to pray. As parents, that's your responsibility. Put Christ back into your lives, He cares. I won't preach to y'all today, I'll let Reverend Clark handle that. Although, I will say to you that a heavy price had to be paid for the vehicle that has brought the opportunities that exist for us today. Many of our people have gone to jail, went through hell, compromised principles, and their convictions, all for the love of you, my black family. Our community is a way for the future, and it will work, as long as we make it work.

Many attempts have been made by our people to become a self-sufficient race, and for many reasons those attempts have been dumped upon, like rubbish landfills. At some point in time, one day, even this attempt may get flushed. I really don't know, but if we learn to love and care for each other, our forging ahead will overcome anything. It really doesn't matter to me, who is blamed for the conditions of our people, because we can deal with our problems, and still not fall prey to a heathen lifestyle. Yet, as I reflect on the past mistakes of black people, an old lady can get pretty riled, but when I see such a promising tomorrow in the palms of our hands, it makes me proud of my people. In our hearts, each of us knows what it's going to take for us to make it from one step to the next. I know that we all have the guts to do it, and Jesus knows that we will. He will order our steps. And since each of us represent something special, I have a special flag to represent our individuality. At this time, I would like to ask the new, E. K. Waymon learning institution's color guards to usher in and display our new community flag, designed with all of us in mind."

Our minister of education stepped back from the podium and our young people's color guard unit entered, carrying a flag displaying red, black, and green, trimmed in a sunburst. After the flag displaying ritual from the color guards was finished, Mrs. Harden returned to her, stone-faced stance at the podium, and decoded the hues of our new banner.

She shouted, "The red, that's for the blood that has been, and will have to be, lost to resist forces that hinder our progress. The color black represents you, me, and other proud men and women that stand fast to create and preserve our communities. The color green, that's the reward of the land that we are blessed to build upon, Mother Earth. Finally, the band of gold that borders the three colors shall serve as a reminder of how God has let His Son, and the sun, shine over us all. Our people will stand proudly under this banner that displays the colors of our liberation. Let us understand that we are working on the assumption that a peaceful world is within reach, accompanied by a satisfactory standard of living. It is not for the asking, and not to be served up on a silver platter, or begged for; earning it is all of our responsibilities. The formula for achieving peace, and all of the other amenities that it includes, will begin according to the law of the land. First, plant a seed from within, then know your own self worth, and derive a mathematical equation that will breed an awareness to offer you a peace in your mind. This equation equals equality, and harmony among all. This is how we can all live and achieve, in spite of our situations, rather than living and existing complacently, despising our situations. Remember that life is for learning, and knowledge is the main ingredient for producing a unique and creative individual, a route to a brighter tomorrow. Our communities must adopt this attitude for the future's preservation.

Before I close, I want to share something else with you that I think will give us food to help feed our appetites for developing a sense of pride. We carry over the name, E. K. Waymon, from our original learning institution. We also carry an error that was made by that administration, and those that followed. Eunice Kathleen Waymon wrote our original school's song, but it was disallowed because of expected complaints from some that believed the song would stigmatize our school. Today, we are proud people who are not ashamed, but ever ready to represent, and to be represented. We will save our own children, provide for, and teach them. That is the charge of this village community. Ladies, gentleman, and young adults, your school and community's anthem, "To Be Young, Gifted and Black." This is the song that we must sing, and teach, for generations to come. Finally, please allow me to thank you all for your time, and your patience. May God bless."

I was very proud of our minister of education. With tears in her eyes, she'd spoken of so many things that most in attendance had never thoroughly considered before. She made us realize that black love, is black wealth. Her words had been an education of their own merit. It was also a pleasing feeling to know that Black people had a restored village to live in. We now have a place where we can plant, and grow the seeds that Mrs. Harden had given us through her wisdom, a place where we can cultivate our culture. For the results that presented themselves to me, I make no apology to any man for the many questionable ways that had to be used to achieve such results. However, I did make my peace with God, for the wrong doings that I'd conveniently justified, as acts governed by an unwritten code of war for warriors.

As time passed, the benefits of Mrs. Harden's oration became apparent throughout our communities. Although for me, the happiest days came when I started on another proposal. In my heart, I knew of only one other thing that I could contribute to the world. Just as before, Regina, and Bert, was to be key figures in the success of that venture too. I had matured enough to understand that in order to adequately prepare for the world's future; I must select a lifetime mate, reproduce, and teach my offspring the ways of life. In my heart, that was a void that could only be filled by one. I asked Regina's hand in marriage, and proudly, she honored me by agreeing to become my bride. My longtime homeboy Bert, he was to be my best man!

The wedding bells sounded and Mama, Evelyn, my nieces Estelle and Clara, along with my brother-in-law Daniel, all attended our ceremony, and welcomed Regina into our family. For her and me, the gathering brought forth a union of years together as husband and wife in loving happiness. She and I bought a mansion on the newly developed west side; it was truly a time for us to savor the flavor of our fruit. Together, we tasted the nectar reaped from the seeds that we had planted. Soon, the bountiful times of joy between her and I were escalated into a treasured elation, with the birth of our first son, David. He was a strong and beautiful infant, blessed with God's breath of life. He was my finest contribution to the world, a gifted, black man-child. I was proud of him, and that's a fact. Mama shouted, Hallelujah! She praised God for grand-baby, number three.

Life had truly shown itself to be, a never ending cycle. It's truly a growing and learning experience. Through it all, I'd done many things that I wasn't very proud of, but I'd done more things that I was proud of. Although, I might not ever be able to proclaim to be a model citizen, I will profess to always doing the best that I can to become one. I've learned that the innocence of my heart will always guide my future, because I try to be as close to God as I can. He is my leader, and I'm His agent. In Him, I'm also mankind, and I'll govern myself accordingly. This is my stance, and it will allow each of us who obtain such a mentality, the opportunity to become much more than what society considers a good American citizen. It will truly make us productive citizens of the world. If we approach life with such a mentality, it's also conceivable that one day, we may all become universal citizens in peace. We can all be good citizens of the universe because the contents of the universe make up a God given dessert. There's plenty for everyone, and it's intended for each of us to enjoy our piece of the pie. But, we must always remember, never take a bite from someone else's slice.

I sincerely hope that no one ever pinches me, because the reality of a village community for my people, is one dream that I hope never comes to an end.